D<small>ETERMIN</small>  1

PETRIFIED WORLD

YOU ARE THE HERO OF THIS BOOK!

WRITTEN BY
JEFF STORM

ILLUSTRATED BY
HARVEY CHAN

EDITED BY
KAROLINA BRYNCZKA

CCB Publishing
British Columbia, Canada

Petrified World, Determine Your Destiny No. 1:
You Are the Hero of This Book!

Copyright ©2009, 2014 by Jeff Storm
ISBN-13   978-1-77143-159-0
Second Edition

Library and Archives Canada Cataloguing in Publication
Storm, Jeff, 1972-, author
Petrified world, determine your destiny no. 1 : you are the hero of this book!
/ written by Jeff Storm ; illustrated by Harvey Chan. -- Second edition.
ISBN 978-1-77143-159-0 (pbk.).--ISBN 978-1-77143-160-6 (pdf)
Additional cataloguing data available from Library and Archives Canada

Illustrations and cover artwork by: Harvey Chan

Publisher: CCB Publishing
             British Columbia, Canada
             www.ccbpublishing.com

Reviews from Young Readers

"*Petrified World* is a powerful book that is packed with action and suspense! This amazing book makes me wonder what will happen to me in the adventures ahead." - *Maja, 12 years old*

"I enjoyed reading it, very clever concept. Great introduction, entire story was well thought out. After each decision the story became even more exciting!" - *Mack, 14 years old*

"The book *Petrified World* is an action and thrilling story that you can't put down until you are done with the mission. In this book you will act as a hero and save the land of Zaar from the evil Darkblade. I was attracted to this book because of the exciting action parts, awesome word choices, and great pictures. Over all this was an action packed exciting book." - *Jianing, 11 years old*

"I thought the book was amazing! It's not like an ordinary adventure book. In every section there's a new thrilling challenge that comes your way. To reach the end of this book I must have died at least 6 or 7 times. The book is great because it's exciting and when I read this book, I felt like I was actually in a magical land. I also loved this book because before you start your adventure it tells you your life story. It's the best book I've ever read." - *Madison, 11 years old*

"A truly fantastic work of words. The characters seem to come alive and guide you throughout the story. Perfect for a person who loves adventure, magic, and choosing their own way, knowing that the outcome is entirely in their hands." - *Sarah, 10 years old*

"*Petrified World* is a breathtaking book. As soon as you read the first page, your head fills with amazing images. This book could be your life story, so flip through these pages and enjoy." - *Sara Jane, 10 years old*

"As soon as I start reading the book, I feel like I am right in this thrilling and magical world. The book is simply amazing and full of rich descriptions. *Petrified World* is a really great book to read!"
- *Alathea, 10 years old*

"I love *Petrified World*; it captured my interest right from the beginning. It has really cool pictures and it's very hard to win! I highly recommend it!" - *Thomas, 10 years old*

"A well-crafted magical story that will pull you through the pages as if you were Darkblade's next victim. So, will you enter a petrified world? Remember whatever you choose determines your destiny."
- *Danielle, 11 years old*

This book is dedicated to all the brave warrior readers
daring to jump into this great adventure,
especially my children Johan and Paulina.

As well, to my wonderful wife Karolina:
thank you for your initial and ongoing support,
for believing in me and for your marketing savviness.

Good luck to all!

Your mission is no easy task but
challenge your imagination
in order to complete this magical journey!

Hey Jai!

Watch out

for Darkblade!

Jeff Storm

HOW TO READ THIS BOOK

This is no ordinary book that you simply read by flipping the pages one after the other. You will travel through the book, going back and forward to complete your mission. At the end of almost every section, you will have to make a choice regarding what you want to do or where you want to go. Only YOU can make such decisions, but you must know that every one of your choices can be either excellent or fatal for you. If you die, your mission officially ends. At that point, in order to complete your mission, you can start reading the book from the beginning again, or simply go back to the section before you died and make a better choice of action.

Your mission is no easy task, so get ready to rumble and fight for those who need you…and try to stay alive!

YOUR STORY

Everybody has a story to tell. But your story is like no other. It is almost from another world. This story is in every molecule of your body and has changed your life forever. It will stay in your soul for eternity…It is who you were destined to become and who you will always be.

It started years ago. You were on your way home, coming back from a trip to China, on board flight 779. Suddenly your plane tipped forward and started to free-fall above Tibet. You were sitting right by the window, next to the wing, and you noticed the burning engines with horror. But it was too late to panic. Within seconds, a terrible shock split the plane right open, crushing it, pulverizing almost everything inside, killing the crew members and the passengers, and ejecting you out of the aircraft into the freezing night. Before you could realize what was happening, you were thrown down the side of an icy mountain, sliding down at a tremendous speed. Blinded by the blowing snow hurting your eyes, you suddenly crashed against an enormous rock, fracturing the back of your scull. Then nothing. Only darkness.

By means of incredible luck, you were found almost dead in the morning by a group of Tibetan monks. On an improvised stretcher, they rushed you inside their lamasery to try to save you…and they did. You stayed in a coma for a month, but when you finally woke up, you had no memory! Your name, where you came from, everything about you was a deep mystery. The lamasery's High Priest said you could stay until you regained your memory. So you stayed…nine long years!

During those years, you slowly regained your memory, learned to speak Tibetan, and became one of the few privileged people to earn the right to learn various mystical Tibetan arts. You mastered many healing arts, martial arts, and magical arts. Having learned the basics of all magical arts, the High Priest asked you to specialize in five of those arts, telling you that you would master all the other magical arts with time and experience. He also told you to use what you have learned for good purposes only.

You will always clearly remember some of the last words the High Priest said to you: "You have acquired extremely rare and amazing skills. It has now become your destiny to preserve all real life forms, and to help those in need. You must know that if an object is given life through a magic spell, it is not a real life form; therefore if it attacks you, you can destroy it. Now keep in mind that if you can defend your own life or somebody else's because it is threatened, you must do so. But with the powers and skills you have, you can neutralize your opponents using the least amount of force required in order to preserve their life. This last rule does not apply if your opponent is not a real life form. Remember that and go in peace."

After receiving his blessing and thanking him and all the monks for what they had done for you, it was time for you to go back home. You embraced everyone and promised you would be back some day to visit them. Then, trying to hide your extreme feelings of sadness and choking down a tear, you left to a new life…but you will never forget your Tibetan family.

You knocked on your parents' door. It was the first day of Christmas. You will always remember the look on your mother's face when she saw you standing in the doorway. The house full of family and friends went dead quiet and suddenly rushed to the main door when they heard your mother's reaction. Then, nothing but screams, tears, joy, shouts, frenetic hugs, and kisses. Emotions ripped through the air while you were grabbed from everywhere. That Christmas was the best one for your family, and your mother said she would have never expected in a million years to receive such a gift from God.

After entering the house and being bombarded with questions, you told your family and friends what happened to you during the past nine years. But you chose not to say anything about your special training, skills, and powers. You felt they would not understand. Maybe you will tell them some day.

So this is your story. But it is only the beginning…

YOUR MISSION

Zaar is one of the wonderful and magical worlds that exist on our planet, but it belongs to a different dimension, another reality. Its people have always lived happy and in peace with one another, using rudimentary magic to live better lives and help each other. But now a notorious master of black magic named Darkblade threatens the peaceful existence of Zaar. His goal is to become the supreme ruler of Zaar and of the other worlds, even if it means to pillage, to terrorize, to take over people's minds, and to kill whoever gets in his way. He already took over the king's palace, making him a slave. With his wicked red eyes, he took over the mind of the rebellious people who were brave enough to stand up to him, transforming them into deadly soldiers who idolize him. But sometimes he simply chose to kill such rebels. Darkblade is now controlling most of Zaar and also plans to conquer other worlds.

This evil sorcerer must be stopped at once before it's too late. Your exceptional skills and very high level of training make YOU the only one capable of putting an end to his reign of terror. But remember what the High Priest in Tibet told you: "You have to respect and preserve all true life forms." Therefore you cannot take away Darkblade's life. Your mission is to bring him to a master-wizard named Keinu. This master-wizard specializes in the field of memory, extending people's memory to help them live better lives or erasing parts of their memory for therapeutic reasons. Keinu has been contacted telepathically by the High Priest from Tibet and is expecting you. At your arrival with Darkblade, the master-wizard will magically erase all parts of the tyrant's memory concerning a dangerous formula baptized *Black Death* and everything relating to it. For the tyrant, it will be as if he never existed as "Darkblade" but as the man he was before. At the same time, the world of Zaar and its people will be free of all spells that were cast by the wicked master.

You will then travel with Darkblade to the Tibetan lamasery where you spent nine years. There, Darkblade will be offered a new existence, a life he always dreamed of before becoming evil. For him, this new life would mean becoming a very trusted and respected healer druid, strictly practicing the magic of healing under the High Priest's supervision.

During this unpredictable journey, you will have to be extremely careful. Your life will be in constant danger, and you will have to use all your might and skills to decide whom you will be able to trust. Nobody else but you will decide which actions to take, where to go, or who to talk to. Remember that you don't have the right to kill any real life forms. If attacked, you can only destroy objects or things on which a magical spell had been cast.

Your task is an extremely difficult one, and the faith of all the magical worlds is in your hands. It is your destiny to try to save all those people. They know you are coming for them, but so do your numerous enemies! It's up to you now. Try to come back alive. Best of luck!

ABOUT DARKBLADE

Darkblade used to be a druid named Rekken. After losing his beloved brother to a terrible illness, Rekken dedicated his time to create more effective magical potions to fight all kinds of diseases and heal wounds. One night, Rekken had a vivid dream about a potion's formula. That formula gave him the very strong feeling of being capable of healing people forever from all diseases and wounds. When he woke up, he felt extremely excited. He thought that such a dream must have been a sign from his genius subconscious mind. He immediately wrote down the formula on an old scroll and rushed to his lab to make the potion.

At noon of that same day, Rekken announced to the people of Zaar that he had created the perfect potion, capable of healing all diseases and wounds forever. The people of Zaar were thrilled to hear such great news. For this amazing accomplishment, the king of Zaar himself invited Rekken to his palace to reward the great druid by offering him a place to work and a private room inside the palace. But before giving out the reward, the king wanted to see the potion's effects.

Inside the palace, the king asked Rekken to heal one of his old faithful servants who was dying in bed. The druid gave the servant a sip of the magical potion and observed. The servant's face instantly became chalk white, and his breath turned very irregular. A moment later, the poor man was lying dead in his bed. Fearing for his own life, Rekken quickly escaped the king's palace and fled to one of his many hideouts, leaving the furious king behind, yelling, "I will ban you from this world!"

When he arrived to his hideout, the druid tripped on a rock and badly sprained his ankle. But there was no time for whining. Terribly confused about what had happened, Rekken reviewed the formula written on the old scroll. What went wrong? How was this possible? Reading the scroll, the druid suddenly noticed he made a crucial mistake while mixing the potion: he omitted to add a handful of black powder from a crushed tree trunk. "What have I done?" he thought. But an acute pain suddenly reminded him of his badly sprained ankle. "I know what I have done wrong and this time I will not fail," said Rekken. "Let's see what this potion can do for my ankle." Very carefully, the druid mixed together all the necessary ingredients, making sure to use the appropriate amounts.

After a while, when the potion was finally ready, the hermit said out loud: "I have nothing to lose, and with what happened in the king's palace, my life is at stake anyway. This is my moment of truth." He swallowed the potion nervously and almost vomited because of its awful taste. His body immediately started to shake, while he was losing his sight. An incredible force suddenly crushed him down to the floor as he panicked. His entire body was seized with brutal convulsions, and he felt that both his head and stomach were about to explode. The pain he was now feeling was unbearable. He started to scream without control, now completely blind, and he thought he was going to die. He started to cough up blood, and his skin turned flaming red. A tremendous convulsion made him hit his head so hard against the floor that Rekken passed out, lying in his own blood and mucus.

He woke up three days later. When he opened his eyes, his sight was back, and everything around him was a mess, but he was alive. Strangely, he felt extremely strong and energized, like never before. "It worked," he thought. As he jumped on his feet, the atrocious pain in his ankle pulled him right down. That pain opened an unprecedented anger in him, showing him that he was a failure because he did not heal himself. With a terrible fury, he opened his mouth to yell, but instead of a scream, enormous flames came out from deep inside him! Then suddenly, he remembered...

When Rekken was six years old, his father Drel, an old and wise druid, was mixing potions to create a specific antidote for himself. After drinking a new potion, Drel felt terribly sick to the point that he passed out. That day Drel made the same discovery Rekken dreamed of years later during the night. When Drel woke up, he felt incredibly strong and refreshed. He wrote the extraordinary potion's formula on the first page of his magical spells' book and closely observed the way he was feeling. He quickly realized what new fantastic magical powers he had and that those powers could be deadly for others, even lead to the destruction of all worlds. In his book of spells, he chose to enumerate all his new powers under the title "Dark Magic," next to the deadly formula he baptized "Black Death." Then the old druid made the promise to himself to use his magical powers only for the good of everything and everyone.

His son Rekken wanted to become a druid as well and begged his father to accept him as his apprentice. "You will become my apprentice only when you will be old enough and responsible to understand the importance of what druids do," his father told him. Frustrated of always hearing the same answer, Rekken went to his father's secret laboratory when the old man was away, found the book of spells on the main shelf, and instinctively opened his father's book...to the first page! Without understanding what he was reading, the young boy quickly went through the page and, fearing his father's return, placed the book back on the shelf. He turned around to leave and met his father face to face. Drel realized what had happened in his lab and was not pleased at all. "You will never learn from me," he told Rekken. Then the old druid opened his book of spells, ripped out the first page with the Black Death formula and burned it, fearing his son might take another look at it and do something foolish. Nevertheless, it was too late: the damage was done. Rekken's brain quickly forgot everything the boy had read, but his subconscious mind wrote everything down, to the last letter!

Yes, Rekken remembered now. He clearly saw the page entitled "Black Death" in his mind, with all its information about the ingredients needed to create the magical potion and the stunning magical abilities resulting from drinking it. He suddenly realized the amazing powers he had within him and craved for more. Rekken felt like the most powerful man in the universe, like an invincible and almighty God. That feeling made all his deepest angers come out. He screamed in vengeance: "All of you who made my life miserable or showed no real appreciation for my work will now pay...FOREVER!" His monstrous laugh echoed in the night like a terrible death threat as his eyes became flaming red.

MAGICAL SKILLS

During the long and tough nine years you spent in Tibet, you learned many magical skills from the High Priest. Now is the time for you to choose five magical skills that are going to be yours. Choose wisely because once you start your quest, you won't be allowed to change the skills you picked.

1. **Telepathy:** This skill allows you to read people's thoughts and to send them messages with your mind.

2. **Telekinesis:** This skill enables you to quickly move almost any object or person from one spot to another with the power of your mind; you can do so from any distance.

3. **Invisibility:** Becoming invisible at will and in any circumstances can be a real life-saver, especially when you find yourself in front of many dangerous enemies.

4. **Flying:** Mastering this skill allows you to fly like a bird at any height and any speed you want, even at the speed of the mind!

5. **Sixth Sense:** This skill enables you to feel what is the best course of action to take in a given situation, including which way to go when you are on the road. It allows you to feel the presence of your enemies and of any other danger.

6. **Owl's Eyes:** This skill allows you to see as clearly during the night (or in any dark places) as you do during the day, just like an owl!

7. **Heavenly Shield:** This is the ultimate shield of protection; nothing can get through it. By mastering this skill, you can make this shield appear on your forearm at any time and block whatever projectile comes your way.

8. **Eternal Breath:** Mastering this skill means being able to breathe under water for an unlimited period of time.

9. **Fire Jet:** This skill allows you to throw blazing fire jets with amazing precision and power through short and long distances.

10. **Paralysis:** With this skill, you can touch or strike any opponent's vital point and paralyze him, her, or it from head to toe. You can also knock an enemy unconscious with a single finger pressure.

11. **Ice Bolts:** This skill enables you to throw huge bolts of ice with great precision and strength through long and short distances. When the ice bolt makes contact with its target, the entire target becomes completely frozen.

12. **Tight Web:** By mastering this skill, you become able to throw a spider-like web on any enemy. The web magically appears at your fingertips, and when it touches your opponents, it automatically closes on them very tightly, not allowing them to move.

13. **Iron Bolt:** With this skill, you can throw big bolts of iron on a specific target. It is ideal for blasting a heavy door, a very thick wall, or even gigantic artificial life forms.

14. **Molecular Travel:** This skill is rarely used, but it allows you to travel anywhere through Earth, through any magical worlds, and from any world to any other. This type of traveling is always done at the speed of mind.

Here is a little surprise for you: if you complete your mission with success, you will be allowed to add a sixth magical skill to the five that you already have! This means that every time you read a book from the series *Determine Your Destiny* and complete the assigned mission, you can add a new magical skill to your other magical skills. Choose wisely!

YOUR MAGICAL SKILLS

PUT A CHECK MARK NEXT TO THE POWERS YOU CHOOSE

1. Telepathy ☐

2. Telekinesis ☐

3. Invisibility ☑

4. Flying ☑

5. Sixth Sense ☐

6. Owl's Eyes ☐

7. Heavenly Shield ☑

8. Eternal Breath ☐

9. Fire Jet ☑

10. Paralysis ☐

11. Ice Bolt ☐

12. Tight Web ☐

13. Iron Bolt ☑

14. Molecular Travel ☑

1

The feeling of a very intense but pleasant presence wakes you at three o'clock in the morning. All your senses fully awake, you sit on your bed and look straight ahead. You see the High Priest standing in front of you with a big smile on his face. He used the magical art of molecular travel to get to your home to see you and to tell you about your mission. You listen to him very carefully, taking notes in your head of every piece of information he is telling you. Then, the High Priest looks at you seriously and says:

"To reach the magical world of Zaar, go to the forest behind your home and walk towards the North. You will eventually find a small and narrow cave. Enter that cave to find the secret door to Zaar that only you and a few others can open. But remember: be very careful about who you trust. Use your powers and your heart to guide you. On my part, my spirit will be with you."

The High Priest touches your forehead and slowly disappears before your eyes. You are absolutely amazed at what you just heard! Such an incredible mission is given to you in another world, a world of magic parallel to yours but in a different dimension. You feel very honoured by the High Priest and say to yourself, "this is my destiny, my life. With great power comes great responsibility. Therefore I must help those who need me."

With such a long and difficult journey ahead, you know that you have to rest some more, despite your tremendous excitement. You close your eyes, relax your body deeply, and within seconds you are flying through the land of dreams.

You wake up at eight o'clock in the morning. After packing some food and personal items, you eat a solid breakfast and leave through the back door.

You are now outside in your garden. You start walking towards the gigantic forest behind your home, wondering what the future holds for you. "What a gorgeous day," you say to yourself, thinking about the clear blue sky, and the peaceful surroundings. Suddenly you hear a terrible scream ripping through the air, which seems to be coming from behind a nearby bush.

"HELP! PLEASE! HELP ME!"

It's a young woman's voice. At the sound of her atrocious scream, your heart nearly stops beating as your blood almost transforms itself into an icy stream inside your veins.

If you wish to go see who is screaming for help, run to section 3

If you prefer to ignore the scream, walk to section 5

2

Your extremely well developed sixth sense warns you about a great threat nearby. You can feel a presence looking at you, observing your every move. You sense death coming close to you and you cannot stop a shiver from going down your spine. Your life is in serious jeopardy!

Continue your journey to section 4

3

As fast as you can, you run to the nearby bush. Judging from the extremely alarming screams, you think that you will probably have to face several tough opponents. You spring over the high bush to get behind it. To your surprise, you find a young woman, all alone, lying on the ground with a bloody mouth and her eyes closed, now silent as death itself. You quickly approach her and grab her by the shoulders. Immediately you put your ear on her chest to listen for a heartbeat. Suddenly, you stop breathing! In a totally unexpected move, she swung a long knife at your legs, wounding you at the ankles with a thin blade covered with a powerful deadly poison. She then looked at you with her red flaming eyes, the trademark of Darkblade's assassins whose minds he controls. The young woman from Zaar was sent by Darkblade to quickly eliminate you. You don't even have the time to realize your journey is over before it has begun. Zaar and all the other magical worlds are now doomed forever. You have failed your mission, because you are dead.

THE END

4

The forest is very deep and dense. It is actually so dense that in many spots the sun can hardly reach the earth, giving the forest a very sinister aspect. You keep walking towards the North, searching for a small and narrow cave.

"I never expected to look for a cave in such a forest," you say to yourself. "I hope I am walking in the right direction."

A sudden cracking noise behind you makes you quickly turn around. Not far from you, you notice an adorable marmot eating berries from a bush. You smile at the beautiful creature and resume your walk towards the North, reassured that the marmot was not an enemy. Nevertheless, the sense of discomfort you felt before sticks to you like glue, omnipresent in your being.

After walking for about three hours, you finally notice two forms ahead, both made out of rocks, behind gigantic trees.

"The cave finally...but...I was not expecting to see two of them."

As you approach the caves, you notice that the one on your left is quite large and covered with heavy black rocks. The one on your right is small and narrow, covered with yellowish rocks.

"The cave I am looking for must be the small one on my right," you say, remembering its description provided to you by the High Priest. But why is there a second cave? What's inside? Is there another door to one of the many magical worlds? Its shape, size, and color intrigue you. Your natural sense of adventure tempts you to take a look inside.

If you choose to enter the large cave, walk to section 6

If you prefer following your original plan, enter the small cave at section 12

5

A deep feeling tells you to ignore those screams. You resume walking to reach the forest, trying to imagine what the magical world of Zaar looks like. As you reach the forest, a strange feeling of discomfort goes through your entire body, but you are not sure why.

If you mastered the magical skill of the sixth sense, follow your feelings to section 2

If you don't have the above magical skill, continue to section 4

6

"If I am here, I might as well take a quick peek inside this large cave."

As you approach the entrance of the black cave, a wonderful smell of fresh roses hits your nostrils. The smell is coming from inside the cave, which motivates you even more to look inside. You enter the cave, take a couple of steps and in front of you, you see nothing more than a wall made out of red rocks.

"How strange," you think. "There is no passage, just a red wall. And I wonder where the smell comes from."

At that moment your martial arts instincts made you turn around extremely fast. A young woman with a long knife and red flaming eyes stands at the entrance of the black cave. Four giants that appear to be made out of black boulders stand behind her.

"You will never leave this cave alive," she says, looking at you with death in her eyes.

If you possess the magical skill of heavenly shield, run to section 8

If you mastered the magical skill ice bolt, go to section 9

If you don't have the above magical skills, propel yourself to section 10

7

You realize that grappling with those gigantic creatures would be impossible.

"Each one is thicker than a tree. To move them would certainly be out of the question."

As you say those words, one of the giants picks up an enormous rock and starts walking in your direction.

"This is not good," you say out loud.

Starring at you, the giant suddenly lifts his arms up and throws the heavy rock in your direction. Immediately, you jump high into the air, propelling yourself towards the rock, and with a fantastic kick, you pulverize it into pieces. Still in midair, you reach the giant's legs and with one amazing spinning heal kick, you break his legs into tiny pebbles. The creature tumbles to ground with a heavy noise.

"I am not going to wait for them to knock me out with one of those huge boulders."

You quickly launch an attack by jumping very high into the air, over the three remaining creatures blocking the entrance of the narrow cave. You land behind them on the cave, and before they can turn around to face you, another one of your ecstatic spinning heal kicks sweeps the air like lightening and tears off all their heads at once! Before the monsters can fall to the ground, you push them to the side of the cave so they will not block its entrance. You then jump to the ground and walk towards the young woman still lying unconscious.

Continue your journey to section 13

8

You take a deep breath to feel the energy around you and in the air. It's the same creative energy that exists within each life form everywhere. You feel this warm energy penetrating every molecule of your body, filling it up completely. You then direct all this energy around your forearm while executing a large circular movement with your arm. In a blink of an eye, you are holding the impenetrable shield of heaven.

Before giving your astonished enemies the chance to understand what just happened, you propel yourself in the air towards your opponents. With a staggering spring, you jump over the young woman towards two of the giants, kicking one directly in the face and smashing the other one's head with the shield. The amazing strength of your blows breaks them into tiny pieces. The rest of the attackers quickly turn around to face you. Immediately, the two remaining giants pick up and throw huge rocks at you, but you easily deflect them with your shield. They suddenly jump high into the air, expecting to crush you with their heavy feet, but you know better. Imitating the creatures, you jump to meet them in mid air, punching a giant through his upper body and breaking the other one's torso with a powerful hit using your shield. Both giants crumble to the ground, now forming just a big pile of rocks.

You barely have the time to turn around and stop a flying knife with your shield. The young woman just threw it, starring at you with her red flaming eyes. Unexpectedly, she rushes towards you, pulling out a small axe. She aims at your head, but you block the blow with your shield. Fast as lightening, your hand executes a small circle in the air before hitting the woman at the base of her neck. She falls unconscious to the ground.

Continue your journey to section 13

9

You stare at your enemies, focusing on them as a group while opening a huge flow of magic inside of you. You can now feel the ice coming to the surface of your hands. Fast as ever, you unexpectedly throw four tremendous ice bolts towards the gigantic creatures. Each ice bolt reaches a giant, freezing it and pulverizing it at the same time.

You slowly approach the young woman, but you decide not to freeze her. Out of her hands suddenly comes out a big fireball that she throws in your direction, but you easily annihilate her attack by moving your body out of the way. The woman brusquely launches at you and attacks you with vigorous punches and kicks aimed at your head and torso, but she is no match for you. After deflecting every blow, you rapidly wrap her around you like a powerful tornado and throw her on a grass patch nearby. Her body smashes against the ground while her head hits a tree. She now lies unconscious at your feet.

Continue your journey to section 13

10

At the sound of those words, you propel yourself forward, jumping high into the air, almost over your opponents. With an amazing power, you throw each foot in a different direction, kicking two giants directly in their chins, literally pulverizing their heads. Still in midair, you redirect the movement of your body by pushing with your foot against one of the two crumbling giants to reach the other two monsters. You smash into them with force, breaking their lower torso with two great palm strikes.

The young woman looks at you, obviously surprised at such a skill displayed by a person who should now be dead. Nevertheless, she approaches you slowly, like a tiger about to catch its prey. Then, she takes out an axe...and throws it at you! You were already on the ground when she let go of the axe. The weapon plants itself in a tree as you launch forward and grab the woman. With superb dexterity, you hit a vulnerable point behind her ear, applying a strong pressure at the same time with your index finger. It's enough for her to lose consciousness, now lying at your feet.

Continue your journey to section 13

11

Breathing deeply, you look at the giants facing you, blocking the entrance of the cave. Through your breathing you feel a huge flow of magic running inside of you, as your hands almost turn into iron. Without any warning and in very quick movements, you throw four heavy iron bolts at the giants. They were obviously not anticipating such an action on your part, and each one crumbles to the ground, now forming a pile of steamy rocks blocking the cave's entrance. You throw a last iron bolt to pulverize the rocks so you can go through and enter the cave.

Continue your journey to section 13

12

"I am very tempted to see what is inside this large cave, but I am here to accomplish a very important mission. The large cave can certainly wait."

You approach the small and narrow cave, realizing that the door to the magical world of Zaar is right in front of you. You are about to enter the cave when you suddenly feel an imminent danger behind you. In an incredibly fast movement, you turn around, sweeping the air in front of your face with your arm. A long knife that was about to pierce your neck loses its course. At the same time, your other hand grabs the attacking arm, wrapping it around you to vigorously throw your opponent straight to the ground. The throw was executed with such power and precision that the attacker lost consciousness when SHE hit the ground. Yes, it's a young woman who is now lying at your feet. But out of nowhere, four gigantic creatures, apparently made out of black rocks, jump in front of the entrance of the narrow cave, brutally pushing you away from it and blocking your way in. They don't seem very friendly, and a strong feeling tells you that they are ready to do whatever it takes to stop you from going in.

If you have the magical skill of iron bolt, run to section **11**

If you do not have the above skill, go to section **7**

13

Next to the young woman, you notice a scroll in the middle of a pile of pebbles.

"This scroll must belong to her and probably fell out of one of her pockets during the fight," you say out loud.

You pick up the scroll and read it. It's killing contract…and it's about you! It explains who you are and what your mission is. It also orders your assassin to eliminate you before you can reach the world of Zaar. You simply cannot believe your eyes. You are not even in Zaar and already an assassin has tried to kill you.

"My enemies are more clever than I assumed. I must stay on my guard at all times." Around the woman's neck, you notice a pendant on which you can read *Cordelia*. "It must be her name."

After finding a long piece of rope in your backpack, you tightly tie up Cordelia's hands and feet. An idea suddenly merges in your brain: you will take her with you. It is obviously unsafe for you to leave her behind and she could reveal to you some valuable information. You throw her on your shoulders and approach the small cave to enter it. One last glance at the large cave makes you stop.

**If you wish to take one last look at the large cave,
put down Cordelia and take a look at section 14**

If you prefer entering the small cave, continue to section 15

14

Your curiosity wins over you. You put Cordelia down next to the large black cave's entrance and go in. As you penetrate the cave, a wonderful smell of fresh roses hits your nostrils, but after taking a couple of steps forward, you see nothing more than a wall made out of red rocks.

"This is awkward," you think. "There is no passage, just a red wall. And I wonder where the smell comes from".

Instinctively, you touch the wall with your hand. Immediately, the wall moves sideways and you are sucked inside the cave. A feeling of death wraps around you as you fly through the air at fast speed. What seemed to be an eternity only lasts a few seconds. Before you know it, you come out of this black tunnel and hit a heavy rock wall inside a very large grotto.

"I have a bad feeling about this."

You get up on your feet and look around you. In front of you, at the other side of the grotto, you notice a wall made out of red rocks. "It's exactly like the red wall inside the cave's entrance," you think. "Maybe that's the exit." The grotto is empty but immense and is enlightened by big torches all around it. The ceiling is carved in black boulders full of huge holes. To your disgust, you see blood slowly pouring down the walls and dripping onto the hot ground made out of red marble plates.

You start running towards the middle of the grotto, asking yourself if someone lives here or comes here at all. But deep down inside you know the answer to that question, which explains the atrocious feeling of death you are sensing.

"There is nothing more to see in this large black cave. It's one very creepy and disgusting place! Now let's get out of here."

But before you can finish your thought, an army of men jumps out of the ceiling's holes and land all around you, surrounding you in a very wide circle. Each man has long black hair and is wearing a black robe, holding a tall red wand and staring at you with red flaming eyes. The men's skin is white as chalk and their pointy silver teeth seem sharp as razors. A strong feeling tells you that those men are wizards practicing black magic, and that they don't intend to invite you for a cup of tea.

"I am trapped."

**If you wish to try to talk your way out of this situation,
start talking at section 16**

If you want to attack the wizards, launch to section 17

If you want to try to escape, run to section 18

15

With Cordelia on your shoulders, you enter the narrow cave. You can feel the adrenaline mixing with your blood at the thought of soon being in Zaar. Armed with a powerful flashlight, you keep walking straight into the darkness, as the cave becomes more and more narrow.

After walking for about twenty minutes, the path suddenly turns into a very steep slope. There is nowhere else to go but down. You sit down at the edge of the slope, putting the unconscious Cordelia in a sitting position in front of you and pulling her against your chest. With one arm wrapped around her waist and holding the flashlight in your other hand, you let yourself slide down. Your speed rapidly increases as the earth sprays in your eyes and face. The air full of dust makes it more and more difficult to breathe. You keep sliding, eyes closed, holding your breath and wondering when this is going to end. In a big splash, you unexpectedly hit a shallow body of water that stops you from sliding. There is no more slope, only water up to your waist. Everything around is cold and dark.

Something suddenly moves in the water, close to you. It's Cordelia, now fully awake and starring at you with her red flaming eyes. She tries to kick you in the water with her tied feet, but you easily grab her and administer a small pressure on a specific point at the back of her neck. She passes out again. Grabbing her by the feet with one hand while holding your flashlight in the other, you walk forward in the water as you wonder where this passage to Zaar could be.

After a short while, you reach an impasse: there is nothing more than a wall in front of you made out of yellowish rocks.

"Those look like the same rocks which form the cave's external structure," you think.

You put back the electric torch in your backpack and holding Cordelia by her feet, you instinctively touch the wall with your free hand. Immediately, you have to close your eyes because a very bright light fills the entire narrow cave, as your body becomes almost transparent. A second later, you and Cordelia disappear.

Continue your journey to section 19

16

"My name is…"

"Silence!" yells an old wizard. "We know who you are and why you are here. Our master Darkblade warned us about you, and we will make sure that you never become a nuisance to him."

At the sound of his words, a tremendous force hits you from the back, throwing you on the marble floor, burning your skin. You manage to get up and jump high in the air, trying to avoid being hit by more fireballs. As you land, you kick two wizards right in the face, throwing a third one, striking three more with your elbows and feet. Now you can see wizards rapidly closing their circle on you, throwing more fireballs at you from every direction. Suddenly an unbearable heat hits you from behind, burning your neck, and sending you rolling on the floor. Another fireball hits you in the legs as you scream in pain. You understand that there is no way back and no place to hide. For you, it is…

THE END

17

Like a rocket, you propel yourself forward to strike a wizard in the abdomen with your knee. Someone grabs you from the back but you throw the poor man on two other wizards coming to help him. A sudden powerful electric beam lifts you in the air and throws you with force against a burning torch. The fire burns your eyes and blinds you. As you fall onto the marble floor, another electric beam coming from a wizard's wand violently hits you in the chest, paralyzing your entire body with acute pain. In agony, only then do you realize that it's...

THE END

18

Quickly, you assess the situation:

"My chances of survival are slim: I am completely surrounded by at least a hundred dangerous wizards in a closed cave and I have nowhere else to run than outside. The only possible and logical exit I see is to leave the same way I came in, which is probably by touching the red wall not too far ahead. I have to get to it fast, no matter what."

You start running towards the red wall, hoping that it's an exit. You jump very high into the air to avoid being bombarded by fireballs, electric beams, and other nasty rays. As you land on the floor, you propel yourself forward to reach the red wall. You are about to reach it when two tall wizards jump in front of it and throw electric beams at you. You quickly roll onto the floor to avoid being hit. Immediately, you jump into the air between the two men, sending your feet in two different directions, and kicking each man across the face. You hear their jaw snapping as they fall to the floor, completely knocked out. Without warning, a fireball violently smashes into the red wall, slightly burning your ear, but you nevertheless touch the wall. Instantaneously, you find yourself outside the large black cave, next to a still unconscious Cordelia.

"That was too close," you say out loud.

Continue your journey to section 15

19

You find yourself standing in the middle of a stunning forest. Its trees are so tall that you can barely see the tops. Multicolor flowers grow everywhere, even on the trees' trunk. The green grass glows like it was tainted with a magical aura. Creeks and rivers flow abundantly, their water clear like crystal and shiny like this world's perfect blue sky. You take a couple of steps forward, leaving Cordelia behind you in the glowing grass, looking all around you. You notice adorable animals that you've never seen before, all kinds of amazing birds with two, four wings or six wings, and strange but beautiful plants delicately perfuming the air.

"So this is the magical world of Zaar," you say out loud. "I have never seen anything like it. It's more magnificent and perfect than I could ever imagine."

"This world is far from perfect because of people like you!" screams a deep voice close to you. "You are not welcome here, and will never be."

Instantly, muscular men and women appear from behind nearby bushes and trees, surrounding you in seconds. Everyone is wearing nothing more than some sort of kilt with an ample white top, holding either a bow or a wooden club. Among them you notice a very old man, probably their chief, staring at you with disgust. He suddenly yells:

"Say goodbye to Zaar, stranger, because you will now die."

If you wish to attack your opponents before they attack you, launch to section 21

If you want to try to escape, run to section 22

If you wish to talk to them to try to avoid a confrontation, walk to section 20

20

"I come in peace," you say calmly. "I don't know who you are mistaking me with, but I mean you no harm."

You put your hands in the air and slowly turn around in a circle to show these people that you are not carrying any weapon.

"All right, you are unarmed," yells the old chief. "Tell us who you are, why you are here, and where did you get those funny clothes you are wearing."

At that moment, the High Priest's words came to your mind, reminding you to be very careful of the people you trust.

**If you wish to tell the chief your identity and
the purpose of you being in Zaar, walk to section 23**

If you prefer to alter the truth, go to section 25

21

Like a powerful wild animal, you jump into the air toward the old man, but before you can reach him, a thick fishing net is thrown over you, preventing you from moving. You fall to the ground, all tangled up in the heavy mesh. You hear a brief order before strong men and women gather to hit you with their heavy clubs, bruising every part of your body. You cannot move, and you feel paralyzed. You try to cover yourself, but your head suddenly starts to spin. Before you know, it is…

THE END

22

You turn around and try to escape, running in the opposite direction. A tall colossus appears in front of you to stop you, but you easily throw him over your shoulder. At that moment you feel a sharp pain penetrating your left calf. You look and see a small arrow lodged deeply inside your skin. Your head immediately starts to spin as you fall onto your hands and knees. You feel weaker and weaker, not capable of moving. You fall to your side, suffocating. You realize that the arrow inside your calf was dipped in a lethal poison.

"I will not have time to heal myself!"

Your vision becomes blurry and you start sweating in pain. You understand that for you, it's...

THE END

23

"I come from a world called *Earth* and I am here to free the people of Zaar from Darkblade's reign of terror. He knows I am coming, so he sent an assassin to Earth to kill me, obviously wanting to stop me from completing my mission." You point at the now conscious Cordelia lying in the grass. "Darkblade also created and gave life to giant creatures made out of black boulders to eliminate me on Earth." Smiling, you add, "In my world, people dress the way I do, as you can see."

At the sound of your words, you notice that many men and women from the tribe lower their weapons, smiling at you with a flame of hope in their eyes. But the old chief keeps staring at you seriously, almost trying to read your soul.

"This is a very serious claim you are making. You are saying that you are *The Chosen One* who came from the world *Earth* to free our people as well as to save the other magical worlds from Darkblade. Indeed I see a woman tied up, and lying in the grass with red flaming eyes. But as much as I would love to believe you, I am going to need proof of your identity. Rumors say you are a master of magic, capable of amazing accomplishments. Show us what you can do."

If you have the skill of telepathy, walk to section 24

If you master the skill of telekinesis, go to section 26

If you want to demonstrate your magical invisibility skill,
disappear at section 28

If you have the skill of flying, fly to section 29

If you master the sixth sense, go to section 30

If you want to demonstrate your heavenly shield, run to section 31

If you have the fire jet's skill, propel yourself to section 32

If you master the magical skill of ice bolt, go to section 33

If you have the skill of paralysis, walk to section 34

If you master the use of the tight web, go to section 35

If you wish to demonstrate what molecular travel is, travel to section 36

If you have the skill of iron bolt, run to section 37

If you wish to show what the eternal breath skill is all about,
dive into section 38

If you refuse to show the chief what magical powers you have,
go to section 27

24

You look at the chief and say:

"Wise Chief, I ask you to focus hard on a single sentence that you are going to repeat in your head. I will tell you word for word what that sentence is."

Every man and woman starts to laugh, including the old chief as he answers:

"As you wish. I think what you want to accomplish is impossible, but it is your life that is at stake, not mine."

The old man looks at you for a short while, obviously repeating something to himself in his head. Just by looking at a person, your training in Tibet made you capable of knowing almost everything about that individual, including the person's thoughts. Calmly, you look at the chief and say:

"The exact words that you keep repeating to yourself are the following: Are you really *The Chosen One*, or are you just a fool?"

Not believing his ears, the old man opens his eyes widely, slowly catching his breath.

Continue your journey to section 39

25

"Not so long ago I was in a very serious accident during which my head hit an enormous rock. Since that day, I completely lost my memory. So, unfortunately, I cannot tell you who I am or where I come from because I do not remember, to this day."

The old chief listens to your words and says:

"I can always tell when someone is lying. Right now, it's exactly what you are doing, stranger. By lying, you show no respect or consideration for me and my people, and I fear what you are hiding from us."

Out of nowhere, two arrows hit you in the chest, piercing your body from one side to the other. Screaming with pain, you fall backwards and realize that your mission just ended.

THE END

26

You look at the chief and say:

"Watch what I am about to do, Wise Chief."

You point your hand at three men nearby and start focusing on them. Suddenly a strange invisible force starts to lift the men up from the ground as your hand goes up! People around you cannot believe their eyes. You stop the lifting action when the men are high above the ground. You see them hanging in the air, wiggling with fear like little children.

"Put us down!" they yell. "Put us down now!"

The old chief looks at you with amazement.

Continue your journey to section 39

27

The Wise Chief looks at you and says:

"If you refuse to show us your magic, it's because you have none to show. You are a liar and surely a dangerous impostor."

He barely finishes talking when your throat is suddenly pierced by in tiny poisonous arrow. You quickly grab the arrow and pull it out of your skin, but it's too late. You feel the deadly poison entering your bloodstream as your vision becomes blurry. You do not even have the time to realize that it is…

THE END

28

You approach the chief and say:

"Watch me, Wise Chief. I will now disappear before your own eyes."

Everybody around you starts to laugh, obviously thinking you are a fool. Without adding a word, you look deeply into the chief's eyes, as he looks into yours. Slowly, your body starts to become transparent. A few seconds later, your physical body completely disappeared, but you are still standing at the same spot. You take a couple of steps backwards and observe the chief and every one of his people starring with amazement at the place where you disappeared.

Continue your journey to section 39
29

You ask the chief:
"Did you ever see a person flying like a bird?"
"No," the old man answers, "but I have seen people falling like rocks!"
The entire tribe laughs at the chief's comment, looking at you as if you were a fool who fell down from the moon. Without any warning, you take three steps and propel yourself forward, flying high into the air like a powerful bird. You execute some very fancy maneuvers, flying between trees and above the water at tremendous speed, almost touching the grass at times and suddenly catapulting yourself over close mountains. You fly back toward the old chief, and as you land, the entire tribe looks at you in disbelief.

Continue your journey to section 39

30

Suddenly, you launch towards the chief and tackle him to the ground. A second later, a knife travelling through the air smashes into a tree behind the old man, entering the trunk. Immediately, four men from the tribe neutralize the person who threw the knife, trying to kill their chief. That person is Cordelia. She had gotten rid of her ties and obviously does not like the old man very much. The old chief looks at you with amazement; you just saved his life!

Continue your journey to section 39

31

You take a deep breath to feel the energy around you and in the air. It's the same creative energy that exists within each life form everywhere. You feel this warm energy penetrating every molecule of your body, filling it up completely. You then direct all this energy around your forearm while executing a large circular movement with your arm. In a blink of an eye, you hold the impenetrable shield of heaven. Every man and woman from the tribe looks at you in astonishment.

Continue your journey to section 39

32

You stare at a nearby creek, focusing on its clear water, while opening a huge flow of magic inside of you. You can now feel the fire coming to the surface of your hands, making them hot and steamy. Unexpectedly, a gigantic fire jet comes out of your hands and crashes into the crystal water, making an amazing splash! As a cloud of hot steam comes out of your strong hands, the old man and his people stare at you, enchanted and petrified at the same time.

Continue your journey to section 39

33

You take a look at a dead tree on your left, focusing on it while opening a huge flow of magic inside of you. You can now feel the ice coming to the surface of your hands, tickling hem. In an incredibly fast movement, you throw six consecutive and tremendous ice bolts toward the dead tree. A second later, it is totally frozen. You notice that everybody around looks at you without moving as if they were frozen as well, completely speechless.

Continue your journey to section 39

34

You approach two very tall and muscular women standing very close to the chief. Both women appear to be extremely strong, fearless, and powerful.

"If I may," you say to them, looking at one then at the other.

You put both of your hands on one of their shoulders while letting a flow of magic racing through your entire being. You suddenly expel a very heavy paralyzing current out of your hands into their bodies. The women immediately drop to the ground, incapable of moving, staring at the blue sky with an incredible fear in their eyes. But the chief looks at you with amazement.

Continue your journey to section 39

35

"Here is a proof," you tell the wise chief.

In movements fast as lightening, you start describing very precise but strange patterns with your hands as a cloud resembling a fish net appears at the tip of your fingers. Suddenly, you propel yourself high into the air, making a large circle with your arms while throwing a large and shiny net, looking like a spider web, on a group of men and women. When the web touches the group, it immediately closes on them very tightly, not allowing the men and women to make a single movement, almost suffocating them. The chief looks at you with a huge smile on his face.

Continue your journey to section 39

36

You look deeply into the chief's eyes, and he looks into yours. Slowly, your body starts to become transparent and in a flash, you completely disappeared. In amazement, every tribe member starts to search for you without knowing where to look, feeling petrified and excited at the same time. A few seconds later, you appear above them at the top of a tree. You yell the word *Zaar* for them to notice you and look at you. They just cannot believe their eyes. You then disappear again before reappearing in front of the old wise chief.

Continue your journey to section 39

37

Breathing deeply, you feel a huge flow of magic running inside of you. You can now almost feel your hands turning into iron. Without any warning and in two very quick movements, you throw two heavy iron bolts into an empty nearby field, smashing them with tremendous power into the ground. Everybody becomes dead silent, not believing what just happened.

Continue your journey to section 39

38

You ask the wise chief:

"How long do you think a person can stay under water without breathing?"

The old man looks at you and says:

"My best warriors can hold their breath for about four minutes. After that, they surely would die."

"Please observe this," you tell the wise chief as you walk toward a river. As you reach it, you suddenly go down on your stomach and put your head under the water. Your very tough and long training in Tibet taught you to breathe under water forever. You learned to take the water in your mouth and to extract the air from it, filling up your lungs with oxygen while releasing the water and taking more fresh water in. You could breathe like this infinitely if you wish.

Everybody thought you were dead when after about ten minutes, you took you head out of the water and you stood up, looking at the tribe who was now staring at you in disbelief.

Continue your journey to section 39

39

Slowly, the old chief approaches you and, putting his hand on your shoulder, says:

"There is no doubt that you are *The Chosen One*. We are honoured by your presence and will do everything we can to assist you." The old man then prostrates himself in front of you and says: "My name is Dunlop, and I am the chief of the tribe you see. Forgive me for doubting your identity."

The tribe's member began to scream with joy, making unusual sounds, while holding their weapons to the sky.

"They are greeting you," says the chief. "We will now take care of your prisoner if you wish, and would be delighted if you would come with us to our hideout. There is a great deal of information I would like to share with you."

If you wish to accept the old chief's invitation, walk with him and the tribe to section 42

If you prefer to decline his invitation, go to section 41

40

After a good night's sleep in one of the wooden houses, you are invited the next morning to savor a copious breakfast prepared with all kinds of delightful fruits. Once again, the entire tribe is gathered like a big family around a huge fire.

You are still eating when Dunlop the old chief approaches you and sits next to you. He says:

"We must get you some other clothes than the ones you are wearing. If you are dressed like one of us, you will be able to blend in with Zaar's population and will be less visible to your enemies. Remember that most of Darkblade's soldiers have red eyes, which make them easily recognizable, but his specialized assassins, who are also high ranking officers, wear eyes filters, a kind of thin membrane that they put in their eyes to change the color. Those assassins are vicious and blend into any crowd, so be very careful."

"I promise I will be," you reply.

"Every brave soul who ever confronted Darkblade and rebelled against him got killed or eventually had his or her mind taken over by the powerful sorcerer. To do so, he looks at a person in the eyes and recites some magical words. So make sure it does not happen to you."

"I will do my best," you answer.

The old chief continues: "In our world, money does not exist like in your world. Everybody practices rudimentary magic that is taught by the oldest member in every family. Such magic enables us to fulfill our basic needs, like to build a small house using our mind, and to create our own food, water, and clothes.

"What about defending yourselves?" you ask. "Can't you use this magic to defend against enemies?"

"We do not have such magical knowledge," answers Dunlop. "We could defend ourselves using weapons like spears and clubs, but we do not possess the appropriate magical skills to fight. Only Darkblade has such magical knowledge and he partially shares it with his servants for them to serve him better and annihilate or capture any rebels. It's only a matter of time before Darkblade forces everyone to surrender to him…unless you find a way to stop him."

"I will find a way," you reply, thinking over what Dunlop just said.

"When you reach the capital Kholl, you will witness some very disturbing scenes. One of the worst that comes to mind is that every three days, in the capital's main park, families are being torn apart."

Continue your journey to section 44

41

You tell the chief that you really appreciate his offer but you also share with him that a deep feeling tells you to move fast.

"As you wish," answers the old man. "We respect your decision. Keep walking to the South, and by tomorrow you should reach Kholl, the capital of Zaar. You cannot miss it because it is truly gigantic. Be very careful and remember that our destiny is in your hands. Here is some fresh food and water. You will need it to stay strong. Take these clothes as well and put them on to blend with the population of Zaar."

You thank the old chief, and after saying goodbye to the tribe, you head toward the South, leaving Cordelia with the wise chief. You now realize the importance of your mission even more as the chief's words echo in your head: "…remember that our destiny is in your hands."

You walk all day without incident and notice that it is slowly getting dark. You decide to stop and camp for the night. Quickly, you build an improvised shelter made out of thick branches, greens leaves, and rope. You carefully move it between two large trees to avoid being seen by potential enemies. When you finish building your shelter, you can already see the stars in the beautiful sky. After eating and drinking a little, you lie down on a bed of soft green leaves and fall asleep.

Continue your journey to section 43

42

You decide to follow Dunlop and his tribe to their hideout, realizing that you must learn as much about Zaar as possible in order to successfully complete your mission.

After a long walk going towards the North, you and your companions finally reach your destination. Behind a bunch of gigantic trees, you notice a very tall and large wooden wall. It is build with thick tree trunks, deeply planted into the earth, and placed one next to another. In front of you stands a very thick and impressive wooden gate, behind which you see small wooden houses and young children running around.

"It must be the entrance to the hideout," you say to yourself.

After a quick signal from the chief whistling through his teeth, the gate slowly opens. As you and the tribe walk in, everyone in the huge hideout runs to meet you. Then the wise chief yells:

"This is *The Chosen One* who came to save us all." The old man's words are greeted with tears of joy and relief, as you are suddenly surrounded by people and grabbed from everywhere.

"We will prepare a feast in your honour," says the chief. "Tomorrow, I will tell you what you need to know about Zaar. Now make yourself at home, my friend. You can stay among us as long as you like."

He walks away and tells two guards to lock up Cordelia in the hideout's prison, a solid wooden house with bronze bars instead of windows.

That evening is one you will never forget. On massive wooden tables, men and women put a large quantity of fresh and delicious meat while children prepare delectable fruits and vegetables that you've never seen before. Around a huge fire, people eat, dance, and sing at your side while you enjoy a succulent meal. Late in the night, you converse with your hosts, dance with them, play with children, sing with men and women, and laugh like never before.

"I found a third family," you tell yourself. You feel blessed and embraced by life, as if something or someone is watching over you, and you wish this moment would last for eternity.

Continue your journey to section 40

43

Unfortunately, you will never wake up. During your sleep, a very tiny but venomous snake came out of its nearby nest and slowly planted its

 hooks into your thigh. The poison rapidly spread within you entire body, killing you in seconds. You will be remembered and missed. Tears will fall for you…before rivers of blood flow…because of you.

THE END

44

"What do you mean?" you ask with a worried voice.

"Darkblade is an immoral man who loves power and seeing people suffer. Every three days, a team of six guards leaves Darkblade's palace, and flies to Kholl where the main park is. There, from the passing crowd, they randomly choose a family, and force both parents and children to climb and stand on Darkblade's platform."

You look at the old man and ask: "What is that platform?"

"It is a wooden square shaped floor made out of thick beams. It's elevated above the ground where people from a randomly chosen family must stand a wait to be separated from each other and become Darkblade' slaves, unless…"

"Unless what?" You ask, irritated.

"Unless somebody is brave enough to climb on the platform, fight all six guards and win the fight. If you could accomplish this, you would then free the family. But if you would lose, you would first of all be dead and the family would be sent to Darkblade's palace to become his slaves."

Dunlop pauses and continues:

"At the palace, parents and children are separated forever. When adults are captured, they get their mind taken over by the powerful sorcerer, and become his loyal soldiers. Some eventually become specialized assassins. But if parents try to resist Darkblade at all cost, he sometimes chooses to kill them on the spot. Children are kept in the palace's dungeon until they become old enough to surrender their mind to the wicked sorcerer and join his army. If they resist, they are executed in public."

"That is atrocious!" you yell with disgust. "How can someone do such evil deeds?"

"This is why that evil sorcerer must be stopped before we all share the same terrible faith. My tribe and I used to live in Kholl. We fled our beloved capital and came here to protect our families and children from this despot. When we saw you in the forest, we thought you were one of Darkblade's specialized assassins. But as you now know, we were all ecstatic to find out who you are! You must save Zaar from Darkblade or this world and all the other will be doomed…forever."

"Wise Chief, I am ready to give my life for this world and the other ones," you say seriously. "I will soon leave your people to accomplish my destiny."

If you wish to pack your stuff and leave now, get ready and go to section 46

If you wish to stay another day, walk to section 47

45

After thanking the entire tribe for its great hospitality, you run forward and suddenly jump towards the eternal blue sky, propelling yourself high in the air to the tribe's great amazement. After waving to them from high above, you make a loop and fly towards the South, delighting your eyes with an extraordinary sight underneath you.

"I am not going to fly too fast to stay aware of what I see," you say to yourself.

As you fly very high above the ground, you notice many groups of beautiful birds flying everywhere around you. A sense of love and joy fills your heart as you see those amazing creatures gliding through the sky as if they were angels protecting you in your endeavor. Some birds are tiny and colourful, others are gigantic and white, using two, four, or six majestic wings to fly. When you look down, you see adorable animals jumping here and there, feeding on grass and wild berries or playing together in the shiny green pastures.

"What a beautiful world."

After flying for a while, you notice a small lake ahead of you. It grabs your attention because although there is no wind, its water seems very agitated. You reduce your speed and fly down above the lake to take a better look at this unusual phenomenon. Brusquely, strange shapes spurt out of the water, and climb the sky in your direction. In astonishment, you realize that those strange shapes are gigantic birds made out of water. With their beaks wide open, about ten of them quickly fly towards you while a horrific feeling of death seizes your entire being.

If you wish to talk to the creatures, fly to section 50

If you want to confront them, propel yourself to section 52

46

"If you wish to leave now, come with me. I need to give you something," says Dunlop.

You follow the chief to one of the wooden houses. Inside, a very tall and muscular man hands you a dark pair of pants and an ample white top resembling a shirt.

"Put this on," says Dunlop. "You must blend in with Zaar's population as much as you can." He then takes off his pendant and gives it to you. "This is for you as well. It will bring you luck and might help you in the near future."

Thanking the chief, you take a close look at the pendant. It is a marvelous green jade on a delicate bronze chain. You put it around your neck to Dunlop's great satisfaction.

"It's now time for me to leave," you tell Dunlop. "Thank you for everything."

After packing your backpack, you know it is time to say farewell. The entire tribe came to say goodbye, wishing you all the success in the world. Dunlop approaches you one last time and says:

"My friend, I truly wish you luck. A very difficult journey lies ahead of you. Remember to stay aware of Darkblade's creatures. The wicked sorcerer can create any creature out of anything he wants to build up his army. Now go in peace. You will find Kholl the capital towards the South. We will all pray for you."

If you have the magical skill of flying, fly to section 45

**If you don't or prefer not to fly,
borrow a horse from Dunlop and gallop to section 48**

47

You decide to stay another day to try to retrieve as much information out of Cordelia as you can. Unfortunately, after an entire day of questioning, you did not learn anything at all. Even Dunlop and his people are unable to retrieve satisfying information.

"Her devotion to her master is unbreakable," says Dunlop. "She is under a very powerful magical spell and I believe that only Darkblade could release her from it. Questioning her more would be useless. You need to rest before your departure tomorrow."

That evening, around another huge fire, you once again enjoy the company of your new friends, while savouring some delicious food created by their rudimentary magic.

"Wise Chief," you ask Dunlop, "how is it possible to create food, water, or clothes using rudimentary magic?"

With a gentle smile, the old man answers:

"Rudimentary magic allows you to learn to extract molecules from the air and to condense them into specific shapes and sizes for specific purposes. Our ancestors created that form of magic thousands of years ago to allow people to satisfy their basic needs."

"That is truly fascinating," you say in excitement. "Maybe I could learn it someday."

"Without a doubt," adds the Dunlop.

At the end of another very pleasant evening, you tell your hosts good night and to get some much needed sleep.

Continue your journey to section 49

48

You follow Dunlop to the hideout's barn. Inside, the old man approaches a magnificent white horse, truly the most beautiful creature you have ever seen.

"This is my strongest and fastest horse. I call it Thunder. It's a very loyal and loving animal, and it will take you wherever you want to go. Thunder will greatly appreciate having you as a master."

"Thank you Dunlop. I will take good care of this splendid mount."

After saying your last goodbye to the tribe, you jump on Thunder's saddle and make the animal gallop toward the South. As you ride away, Dunlop and his wonderful people come to your mind.

"Wise Chief, I promise you that I will free you and your tribe from Darkblade. You have my word."

You ride the entire day toward the South, stopping from time to time to rest and drink some water. As the evening starts to fall, you notice a small wooden house and a barn at the entrance of a tiny forest not too far ahead of you.

"Maybe we could spend the night in that barn. What do you think of that, Thunder?"

As a response, Thunder turns his head towards you and approves by neighing.

When you arrive at the house, you find it empty. You look for its occupants to ask permission to spend the night in the barn, but find no one.

"Oh well," you tell Thunder. "I guess people deserted this place. Come on. Let's get some sleep."

You open the barn's door, and as you walk inside with your horse, you find stacks of hay piled up in the right corner in front of you and on the second floor.

"Treat yourself Thunder. You deserve it. We still have a long way to go tomorrow, so eat well and rest. I am now going to sleep."

If you wish to sleep upstairs, jump to section 60

If you choose to sleep downstairs, fall asleep and go to section 68

49

You wake up feeling very energized and ready to go. You go outside and are once again invited to savor a copious breakfast prepared with all kinds of delightful fruits and breads. You talk to men, women, and children about their life in the hideout, their joyful moments, and their fears. With all those eyes looking at you with the deepest hope, you realize once more the importance of successfully completing your mission.

"No matter what it takes, I will complete my mission. Those people depend on me, and I will not let them down," you say to yourself.

After eating and chatting with your hosts, you tell Dunlop that it is time for you to leave.

Continue your journey to section 46

50

"I come in peace," you yell towards the creatures. "I mean you no harm."

You should have trusted the feeling of death you just felt a moment ago. Without any warning, extremely powerful water jets come out of the creatures' beaks and pierce your abdomen from one side to the other. Like a massive rock, you fall down head first into the lake...

Just as so many of Darkblade's victims, you will never be seen again...So many people were counting on you...

THE END

51

You wish to take one last look at the lake from which the water birds came out.

"Maybe I could make some interesting discovery."

You fly down towards the lake to take a better look at it but see nothing unusual. You fly even lower than before and observe its now calm and shiny surface. To your surprise, the water is so pure and clear that you are able to see the bottom of the lake. You see tiny multicolor fish swimming among orange and yellow plankton.

"This is truly beautiful," you say out loud. "It is a shame that such a splendid world is now in jeopardy because of one evil man."

Continue your journey to section 57

52

At tremendous speed, you propel yourself high into the blue sky. You turn around and see the water birds flying far behind you. In an amazing reflex, you tilt your head to the left to prevent a very powerful water jet from penetrating your forehead.

"They leave me no choice," you think to yourself. "I am sure those water creatures were created by Darkblade and will stop at nothing to eliminate me. But today will certainly not be the last day of my life!"

If you master the skill of fire jet, fly to section 54

If you have the magical skill of iron bolt, hurry to section 56

If you don't have the above magical skills, go to section 58

53

You decide to fly at the speed of mind to instantly reach the small mountain behind which the smoke is now becoming more and more heavy. As you land, you notice that the ground is covered with a warm coal dust that seems to be carried by the wind from the other side of the mountain.

Staying low, you run up the gentle slope to the nearby top of the mountain to assess the situation.

When you reach the top, you hide behind a large rock to look down at a scene you would never expect to see. At the bottom of the small mountain, you notice a group of about twenty men and women with red flaming eyes, dressed in red and black uniforms. Each individual is immersing huge swords, spears and other weapons in an enormous pile of red burning coal from which a thick black smoke climbs the sky like a death threat over the world.

"Darkblade's soldiers," you whisper to yourself. "They are probably making weapons for their future conquests."

Among the group you notice one individual dressed in an ample red robe with a hood covering the head and some kind of red cloth covering the face but not the eyes. You hear that individual giving orders to soldiers all around.

"That must be their chief or their captain."

A sudden presence behind you makes you whirl around. You see two of Darkblade's soldiers, a man and a woman, standing in front of you, pointing two spears in your direction.

"Who are you and what are you doing here?"

If you wish to attack them, jump to section 59

If you want to answer their question, start talking at section 61

54

In an instant, you open a huge flow of magic inside of you, feeling the fire coming to the surface of your hands, making them very hot and steamy. Unexpectedly, a burning fire suddenly comes out of your hands as you throw quick and precise fire jets straight at the birds. The huge fire smashes in every water bird with such force that each creature evaporates instantly. Within seconds, all that is left of the water birds is a drizzly mist now falling back into the small lake.

If you wish to fly back to the small lake to take a closer look at it, fly to section 51

If you want to continue flying towards the South, propel yourself to section 57

55

Your sixth sense warns you of a great danger behind the small mountain. You feel the presence of potential enemies, many of them, perhaps an army. Your sixth sense tells you that they are creating something very dangerous, something that can easily take away a person's life.

"I must be extremely careful."

Continue your journey to section 53

56

Breathing deeply, you feel a huge flow of magic running inside your body. You almost feel your hands turning into massive iron. Fast as lightening and with great precision, you throw many heavy iron bolts at the big water birds. Each bolt pulverizes its target in an amazing splash, turning the creature into heavy rain now falling from the sky.

"That wasn't too difficult," you say out loud.

**If you wish to fly back to the small lake to take a closer look at it,
fly to section 51**

**If you want to continue flying towards the South,
propel yourself to section 57**

57

You continue flying towards the South, admiring the wonderful animals, the green forest, the colourful flowers, and the enormous pastures beneath you.

"I could fly at the speed of mind, but again, I don't want to miss anything from this world that is revealing itself to me. What beauty!"

After a while, you notice heavy mountains on the horizon. As you fly closer, a thick smoke coming from behind a smaller mountain grabs your attention.

"How strange," you think. "A thick smoke in this deserted place? Who would live here in such isolation?"

As you fly closer to the small mountain, a bad feeling wraps around your heart like a nasty web.

If you possess the sixth sense skill, fly to section 55

If you don't have the above skill, go to section 53

58

At the speed of mind, with magical precision, you propel yourself forward at the big water birds. With a force out of this world, you pulverize every bird with your body as you smash into each creature's chest, going through it, and coming out of its back in an amazing splash, turning every water bird into heavy rain now falling down into the underneath lake.

"That was refreshing!"

**If you wish to fly back to the small lake to take a closer look at it,
fly to section 51**

**If you want to continue flying towards the South,
propel yourself to section 57**

59

In an extremely fast sequence of movements, your right hand sweeps the spears, breaking them in half as you jump into the air, throwing your legs straight in front of you and kicking your opponents directly in the face. With a loud scream, they crumble unconscious to the ground. You quickly turn around to realize that their scream alerted the rest of the group. All the soldiers are now looking at you, and they are obviously surprised by your unexpected visit. Suddenly their captain yells:

"Bring the intruder to me, dead or alive!"

As soon as those words were said, Darkblade's soldiers begin to run up the gentle slope in your direction.

If you want to fight the soldiers, fight your way to section 63

If you wish to put your hands up and surrender, walk slowly to section 65

If you want to fly away, fly to section 67

60

With no obvious effort, you jump high into the air to reach the second floor, which is quite elevated above the ground. Up there you notice that there are no windows, only a wooden ladder nailed to the left wall joining the two floors, and thick layers of hay under a low triangular roof. Exhausted from riding your horse all day, you let your body drop backwards and quickly fall asleep.

A cracking noise wakes you up in the middle of the night. You instinctively open your eyes, your senses fully awake. After a short moment, you hear the same cracking noise again. You realize that someone is climbing the wooden ladder to reach the second floor.

If you have the magical skill of the owl's eyes, run to section 70

If you don't have the above skill, prepare yourself for section 72

61

You answer the soldiers, telling them:

"I am a farmer and I live around here. When I saw the smoke behind the mountain, I thought the nearby forest was burning, so I came to see if it was so."

"You are lying," replied the woman. "You are not dressed like a farmer. You must be one of those scumbag rebels who are against our master. Prepare yourself to die."

Continue your journey to section 59

62

In extremely fast movements, you start describing very precise but strange patterns with your hands as a cloud resembling a fish net appears at the tip of your fingers. Suddenly, you jump high in the air, creating large circles with your arms while throwing shiny nets looking like spider webs on the groups of soldiers around you. When the webs make contact with the soldiers, they immediately close on them very tightly, not allowing the soldiers to make a single movement, almost suffocating them.

After trapping all the soldiers, you propel yourself into the air and fly towards the big pile of burning coal. When you land next to it, you hear a voice behind you saying:

"I guess it's just you and me now."

You turn around and see the soldiers' captain standing in front of you, holding two throwing knives in one hand and a thin sword in the other. You also notice that the captain is starring at you...with blue eyes!

"The captain must be a specialized assassin," you say to yourself.

"I know exactly who you are and why you are here," says the captain. "This will be your last minute in Zaar. Do you have any request before I take your life away?"

"Yes," you reply. "Take off your hood and mask so I can see who is threatening me."

"And for you to see who is going to kill you!"

The captain slowly removes the thick red hood and the thin mask, exposing a beautiful young woman with long straight brown hair, and delicate lips.

"Goodbye...forever!" she says to you.

If you have the heavenly shield skill, run to section 69

If you have the skill of paralysis, go to section 71

If you did not master any of the above skills, prepare yourself for section 73

63

"Dead or alive," you repeat in your mind. "I am definitively not going to be dead!"

You suddenly notice a soldier at the bottom of the gentle slope aiming at you with his taut bow. A split second later, he lets a poisoned arrow fly straight to you. He should have known that such an attack against you is no match for your years of training in Tibet. In a very quick movement, your hand catches the arrow in front your chest, the poison at its end still dripping to the ground.

"No more of this," you say yourself.

Three men brusquely appear to your right and launch toward you. The first man to reach you tries to hit your forehead with a thick sword. Instinctively, you sweep the attacking arm to the side and push the man down the mountain with your other hand. The two other men try to stab you with sharp knives but are thrown to the ground with great power. Simultaneously, you feel enemies all around you, closing in on you.

If you master the use of the tight web, hurry to section 62

If you have the skill of ice bolt, run to section 64

If you did not master the above skills, jump to section 66

64

You feel your opponents closing in on you, but they do not suspect that you are opening a huge flow of magic inside of you. You can now feel the ice coming to the surface of your hands, tickling them. In incredibly fast movements, you start spinning while precisely throwing huge ice bolts at the soldiers around you. The poor soldiers do not even have the time to realize what is happening to them. Within seconds, Darkblade's loyal servants are all completely frozen, standing like statues.

You then propel yourself into the air and fly towards the big pile of burning coal. When you land next to it, you hear a voice behind you saying:

"That was an impressive display of skill. Let's see what you will do against me."

You turn around and see the soldiers' captain standing in front of you, holding two throwing knives in one hand and a thin sword in the other. You also notice that the captain is starring at you…with blue eyes!

"The captain must be a specialized assassin," you say to yourself.

"I know exactly who you are and why you are here," says the captain. "This will be your last minute in Zaar. Do you have any request before I take your life away?"

"Yes," you reply. "Take off your hood and mask so I can see who is threatening me."

"And for you to see who is going to kill you!"

The captain slowly removes the thick red hood and the thin mask, exposing a beautiful young woman with long straight brown hair, and delicate lips.

"Goodbye…forever!" she says to you.

If you have the heavenly shield skill, run to section 69

If you have the skill of paralysis, go to section 71

If you did not master any of the above skills, prepare yourself for section 73

65

You put your hands up and say:

"I come from Kholl, Zaar's capital, and I have a very important message for your captain. Bring me to him."

The soldiers hesitate. You feel that they want to kill you and that they don't trust you whatsoever. But a powerful voice coming from below says:

"Bring the trespasser to me."

Two strong soldiers, a man and a woman, grab you by the arms and pull you down the slope with them, walking very fast. They bring you to their captain. You notice the captain starring at you…with blue eyes!

"This person must be a specialized assassin," you think to yourself.

You open your mouth and say: "I come from Kholl and…"

"Silence," replies the captain. "Unlike my soldiers, I know who you are and why you are in Zaar."

The captain makes a gesture with his right hand, and you see ten soldiers aiming at you with taut bows armed with deadly poison arrows.

"Listen to me," you say, "I am…"

"I know," replies the captain. "You were alive…but now you are dead!"

In an amazing reflex, you catch three arrows about to pierce you and avoid six others aimed at your upper body. But the last arrow enters your thigh. In a scream of pain, you fall to the ground, dizzy and suffocating. Before you can do anything, the arrow's poison drips inside your veins, poisoning your entire blood stream. To your enemy's great satisfaction, this is where your mission ends.

THE END

66

You sit on the ground in a meditative position and wait for your opponents. Within seconds they surround you. You notice the surprise on their face when they see that you are putting yourself in such a vulnerable position and that you are not even trying to escape. That moment of surprise is your cue...

Abruptly, you jump very high into the air toward a group of soldiers. Faster than a tornado, your hands and feet become extraordinary weapons, precisely kicking and striking your opponents all around you, throwing them to the ground and using their strength against them. Bodies bend and fly in every direction, and enemy hands are disarmed, but you know how to defend yourself in order not to kill any opponent. A moment later the men and women from Darkblade's army lie unconscious at your feet, their weapons next to them on the warm and dusty ground.

Leaving the unconscious soldiers on the ground, you propel yourself into the air and fly towards the big pile of burning coal. When you land next to it, you hear a voice behind you saying:

"I said dead or alive. It's going to be death for you."

You turn around and see the soldiers' captain standing in front of you, holding two throwing knives in one hand and a thin sword in the other. You also notice that the captain is staring at you...with blue eyes!

"The captain must be a specialized assassin," you say to yourself. "Let's be careful."

"I know exactly who you are and why you are here," says the captain. "This will be your last minute in Zaar. Do you have any requests before I take your life away?"

"Yes," you reply. "Take off your hood and mask so I can see who is threatening me."

"And for you to see who is going to kill you!"

The captain slowly removes the thick red hood and the thin mask, exposing a beautiful young woman with long straight brown hair, and delicate lips.

"Goodbye...forever!" she says to you.

If you have the heavenly shield skill, run to section 69

If you have the skill of paralysis, go to section 71

If you did not master any of the above skills, prepare yourself for section 73

67

As you jump into the air to fly away, Darkblade's soldiers shoot poisoned arrows at you. With great agility and speed, you make loops through the air to avoid being hit. The arrows do not have much chance to reach their target. Unfortunately, one does.

THE END

68

You place many layers of hay on the barn's floor as you watch Thunder devouring the hay piled up in the right corner.

After comfortably lying on your back, you take a last look at your hungry companion and close your eyes to get the needed rest after an exhausting day.

A squeaking noise suddenly wakes you up in the middle of the night. Your senses totally alert, you pay attention to hear anything suspicious. A second later, you hear the same squeaking noise once again. You realize that someone is opening the barn's door to get inside.

If you have the magical skill of the owl's eyes, run to section 74

If you do not have the above skill, prepare yourself for section 82

69

You take a deep breath to feel the energy around you and in the air. It's the same creative energy that exists within each life form everywhere. You feel this warm energy penetrating every molecule of your body, filling it up completely. You then direct all this energy around your forearm while executing a large circular movement with your arm. A second later, you hold the impenetrable shield of heaven.

Facing the captain and holding your shield, you can see astonishment in her eyes. The last thing she expected was to witness such an impressive shield to magically appear in your hand. But you know it is not over yet. In two rapid movements, the young woman throws one knife at your legs and the other at your head. You easily deflect both knives with the heavenly shield. Quickly, you pull out a heavy steel axe from the pile of coal as your opponent rushes in your direction, brandishing her thin sword. She is about to reach you when you suddenly throw your weapon to the ground! Totally flabbergasted by such an unexpected move, the woman freezes for a moment, staring at you with disbelief.

"That's my cue!"

In a dazzling spring, you propel yourself forward, and tackle the woman with your shield. The captain falls heavily backward, hitting her head against your shield, and losing consciousness.

Continue your journey to section 133

70

During your intense years of training in Tibet, you learned to see very clearly through the night, enabling your eyes to pierce the thickest darkness wherever you are. You tilt your head toward the wooden ladder and let your eyes do the rest. Suddenly, a man appears at the top of the ladder with a rope in his hands, followed by a woman holding a wooden club. They search the darkness for while, not able to see where you are. Then they notice your body lying in the hay not too far from them. Very slowly, trying not to make any more noise, the couple silently walks in your direction, carefully measuring each step.

If you wish to talk to the couple, open your mouth to section 75

If you want to launch a surprise attack at them, launch to section 77

71

The young captain suddenly throws two sharp knives at you, but you easily catch the weapons in mid air before they pierce your chest. Surprised by your amazing skills, the woman pulls out two small bronze axes from the pile of coal and throws them at you in two very quick movements, hoping to slice you. Once again, your reflexes prove to be superior as you move your body around the flying weapons.

"Now my turn," you tell the young woman.

With great speed, you jump into the air, launching forward at the same time. As you land just in front of the captain, you strike her with your index finger under her nose. At the same time, you let a flow of magic race through your entire body before expelling a very heavy paralyzing current out of your index finger into the woman's brain. She immediately drops to the ground, incapable of moving, staring at the blue sky with incredible fear in her eyes.

Continue your journey to section 133

72

The thick darkness of the night makes it impossible for you to see who is coming or to determine how many individuals are there. Without moving, you make an intense effort to see shapes in front of you, but your eyes can't seem to get accustomed to the darkness. Suddenly you hear a tiny whisper to your right.

"Over here," says a voice.

A short moment later, you notice two human forms standing above you, holding long objects in their hands. The two individuals obviously think you are asleep.

If you wish to talk to them, open your mouth to section 76

If you want to launch a surprise attack, jump to section 79

73

Ready to defend your life, you calmly take a low fighting stance. With a creepy smile on her face, the young captain begins to walk in your direction, pulling out her thin sword from its sheath. But before she can reach you, a small rock suddenly hits her on the side of the head with such force that the woman instantaneously collapses in front of you, completely knocked out by the powerful blow.

"What was that?" you say out loud. "Somebody just saved my life!"

Continue your journey to section 133

74

During your intense years of training in Tibet, you learned to see through the darkest nights, enabling your eyes to pierce any extreme darkness and to see as clearly as you do during a sunny day. You look towards the door and let your eyes do the rest. From behind the door, human forms slowly appear. You notice a young man holding a rope, followed by a young woman with a wooden club in her hands and two small children staying behind. The couple take a while to get accustomed to the thick darkness, obviously looking for you. When they finally see your body lying in the hay, the man and the woman slowly approach you, trying not to make any noise.

If you wish to talk to the couple, open your mouth to section 78

If you want to launch a surprise attack at them, launch to section 80

75

"One more step and you will be sorry to have come near me," you say, still lying on your back looking straight at the couple.

The man and the woman immediately stop walking towards you, not expecting to find you awake. On their face you can now read a tremendous fear paralyzing them. You jump on your feet and say:

"Drop your weapons in front of you."

The couple simply stand there, motionless.

"I am not going to ask you again," you say with a serious voice.

The couple throws the club and the rope in front of them, and the woman falls down to her knees.

Continue your journey to section 81

76

"Step back right now if you know what's good for you," you tell the two individuals.

Not expecting to find you awake and obviously scarred, the two individuals abruptly turn around and run towards the wooden ladder to get down as fast as they can. You beat them to it by jumping down to the first floor.

Quickly, you run to open the barn's door, trying to get some moonlight inside. You turn around and run back towards the ladder, but to your great surprise, there are now four individuals in front of you instead of two: a young couple and two children.

Continue your journey to section 81

77

You jump to your feet and launch at the couple, tackling both of them to the ground at the same time. The man and the woman drop their weapons and fall into the thick hay. In a fast movement, you easily apply an arm lock to both of them, noticing their young eyes staring at you, in which you read a terrible fear.

Continue your journey to section **81**

78

"Stop right there," you tell them.

You can see astonishment on their young faces as they stop progressing in your direction.

"You can drop the rope and the club in front of you. I am no threat to you or to your children."

The couple just stand motionless, paralyzed with fear.

"I am not going to hurt you," you say with a soft voice. "I came here to help."

The couple throw the club and the rope in front of them, and the woman falls down to her knees.

Continue your journey to section **81**

79

From your lying position, you unexpectedly lift your upper body towards the individuals' legs, grabbing them with both of your hands while pushing forward with your chest. The man and the woman softly land on their backs onto the thick layers of hay. Rapidly and with great agility, you turn both of them onto their stomach, still holding onto their legs and applying ankle locks. You feel a deep fear running through their young bodies as their breathing becomes irregular.

Continue your journey to section **81**

80

You keep lying in the hay with your eyes half open, observing the man and the woman slowly progressing towards you. Suddenly, the man rips the club out of the woman's hands and rushes at you, brandishing it above his head. Rapid as the wind, you jump to your feet and deflect a blow to your head as you throw the young man against the stack of hay. A second later, the man simply finds himself sitting on the ground with a sore buttock.

Continue your journey to section 81

81

"Please do not hurt us or our children," says the woman. "We beg you not to harm our family, nor to separate us from one another. All we have left is each other."

A wave of relief suddenly fills you as you step back and say:

"Please do not be afraid. I am not one of Darkblade's soldiers. As you can see, my eyes are not flaming red." Feeling you can trust the couple, you continue: "I mean you no harm. I came to this world to deliver it from Darkblade's tyranny, and I entered your barn to get some sleep. You and I are on the same side."

An expression of hope appears on the woman's face as she says:

"Montar...this individual is the person everybody is talking about: it's *The Chosen One*!"

But the man she called Montar violently replies:

"No! Do not listen to those blasphemous words, Gerda! As far as we know, this person could be one of Darkblade's special assassins."

Looking at Montar, you calmly say:

"If that would be the case, I don't believe I would take the time to talk to you in the middle of the night. You would all probably be dead by now."

Instinctively, you reach for the pendant around your neck given to you by Dunlop and show it to the couple.

"This was given to me by Dunlop. I met him and his tribe, and had the great privilege of being their guest of honour at his hideout."

When he sees the pendant and hears your words, Montar falls to his knees and says:

"Forgive me for doubting you, master, and thank you for coming into our lives."

Continue your journey to section 83

82

The night is so dark that it makes it impossible for you to see who is entering the barn or to determine how many people are there. You force your eyes to pierce the darkness, but they do not want to reveal you anything.

As the barn's door suddenly opens wide, allowing the moonlight to bring some light inside, you abruptly notice two human forms standing above you. Thinking you are asleep, they bend over you and reach out with their hands as if they wanted to grab you.

If you wish to talk to them, open your mouth to section 84

If you want to launch a surprise attack, launch to section 86

83

With a preoccupied expression on her face, Gerda slowly approaches you and says:

"With our children, my husband and I fled our beloved capital Kholl with great difficulty and came here to my grand parents' abandoned property. We did not want to be separated from one another. We hoped that the saviour everybody calls *The Chosen One* would come, and set us free from Darkblade."

"I came from the word called *Earth* to help the people of Zaar and of the other magical world against Darkblade. I will do what I can to stop him before he spills more tears and blood, and I will be on my way tomorrow morning."

"You need to rest now," says Montar. "We promise not to disturb you anymore. Get some sleep, and join us in the house tomorrow morning for breakfast."

You thank your new hosts, and go lie down next to Thunder in the thick hay, closing your eyes, and abandoning yourself to the world of dreams. The rest of the night is quiet, only disturbed from time to time by a singing cricket.

You wake up with the sunrise, rested and ready to go. You leave the barn and walk to the small wooden house where the family of four is already putting delicious food on the table. After mutual greetings, you all enjoy a nice healthy breakfast. The young couple tell you about the existence of a good old lady wizard living nearby in the West, practicing strange magic, and helping many families to hide from Darkblade and his army.

"Darkblade's soldiers patrol this area," says Montar. "Every time they do, we are warned in advance by the old lady who appears in front of us out of nowhere to tell us to hide in our underground bunker. She helped us many times. We were afraid of her at first, but we now know that she is some kind of good wizard."

"She probably mastered molecular travel," you say to yourself. "I wonder where she learned it, and what else she mastered."

After the delightful breakfast, you thank your hosts for everything and tell them you have to leave. You all go to the barn where Thunder eats hay and say goodbye to one another.

"We will be with you in our thoughts," says Gerda. "Take good care of yourself, and try to stay alive."

"I will," you reply while mounting Thunder. "The wind is on our side."

If you wish to continue riding towards the South, go to section 85

If you wish to ride towards the West to see if you could find
the old lady wizard, go to section 87

84

"Don't even think about it," you say with a threatening voice. "Step back right now."

Totally caught off guard by you being awake and so calm, the two individuals turn around in panic, and start running towards the barn's door. You quickly get up and jump high over the runaways in front of the door, annihilating any possibility of escape. Something moves to your right as you hear running noises going towards the two runaways. Thanks to the moonlight, you are now able to see who is standing in front of you: a young man holding an adorable little girl and a woman hugging a boy.

Continue your journey to section 81

85

You propel your horse forward, realizing how fate has helped you so far by putting all those amazing people on your path.

"Let's hope that we will keep having positive encounters, right Thunder?"

Once again you ride all day, stopping once in a while to rest and eat. The beauty of the nature around you truly takes your breath away. You smell the delicate scent of fresh flowers and feel the sweet wind wrapping your face as you admire tiny animals feeding all around you and playing with one another.

In the late afternoon, you notice a thick column of black smoke at the horizon, slowly climbing the sky from behind a small mountain.

"I have a bad feeling about this. A thick smoke like that is never a good omen."

Thunder suddenly turns around to face the small forest right behind you.

"Don't worry Thunder," you say to reassure the animal. "I feel a presence as well."

As you said those words, four men dressed in red and black uniforms and armed with strange swords appear out of the forest. They run towards you and form a circle around you and Thunder.

"By the authority given to us by our master Darkblade, we put you under arrest for trespassing," says the tallest man. "Get down from your horse and come with us."

If you wish to obey, get off your horse and go to section 90

If you want to neutralize the soldiers, jump to section 88

86

You grab the hands that are about to grab you and twist them to make the two individuals roll to the ground. Totally in control of the situation, you easily apply a wrist lock to both of them, noticing their young eyes staring at you. You read a terrible fear in their eyes.

Continue your journey to section 81

87

After waving to the family one last time, you decide to ride toward the West to try to find the lady wizard.

"Who knows," you tell Thunder. "I may learn something of great importance that could help me in my mission."

After a short while, you begin to feel lost, not really knowing where you are supposed to find the wizard.

"Where are you, lady?" you say out loud. "I need your help."

"I am right here," says a soft voice on your right.

You turn your head towards where you heard the voice and see an old lady dressed in an immaculate white robe, standing with a smile on her face. You calmly look at her, not knowing where she came from and impressed by her sudden appearance at the exact moment you called her. But before you can say a word, the wizard says:

"I now know who you are, where you come from, and what your mission is. Your task is almost impossible. But if you trust your instincts and your abilities, you will be successful. Do not fear anything or anyone. Remember that, because it is key to a successful mission. This is all that I can say to you."

You barely have the time to open your lips to ask her a question when she vanishes in front of your eyes, leaving you alone with your thoughts.

"Trust your instincts and your abilities," you repeat to yourself. "I need to know more than that, but I guess it will have to do. Let's go, Thunder!"

Continue your journey to section 85

88

From your sitting position, you jump forward into the air, executing a split and kicking two men directly in the face at the same time. Seeing what was happening, Thunder suddenly leans forward on its front legs and kicks the other two men, smashing its hoofs into their jaw. The soldiers hit the ground like heavy boulders.

"Good job," you tell Thunder with admiration in your voice. With a loud neigh, the animal trots to you, and licks your hand. "I say we get out of here. I am sure there are other soldiers patrolling this area."

A burning smell makes you turn your head and stare at the small mountain for a moment.

"What is that nasty smoke?"

If you want to find out where the smoke is coming from,
saddle up and tell Thunder to take you to section 93

If you prefer to ignore the smoke,
ride around the small mountain to section 95

89

You agree to follow the soldiers to their captain.

"Maybe I could learn something more about Darkblade," you tell yourself.

You see one of the soldiers slowly approaching Thunder, measuring the steps to jump on its back. Abruptly, the beautiful creature turns around and kicks the soldier right in the abdomen, knocking the air out of him, and crushing his ribs. Furious, two other soldiers pull out their swords to slice the animal, but in a dazzling spring, you launch towards them to strike the back of their neck with the side of your hand. The two men crash face first into the grass. You turn around and see the tallest soldier staring at you with disgust.

"Let's find out what you can do against my sword," he says angrily.

He rushes at you, aiming for your throat with the tip of his sword. Vivaciously, you tilt your head and step to the side, avoiding the weapon while grabbing your opponent's wrist and twisting it against the joint. The man's body flips through the air before smashing with amazing power onto the ground. You look at the now unconscious man and tell Thunder:

"Let's get out of here before we face more trouble."

**If you want to find out where the smoke is coming from,
saddle up and tell Thunder to take you to section 93**

**If you prefer to ignore the smoke,
ride around the small mountain to section 95**

90

You obey the soldiers and jump to the ground. They quickly search you but do not find anything of interest.

"Who are you, what are you doing here, and why are you trespassing?" asks the tallest of the soldiers. "Nobody is allowed to leave Kholl without a written permission from a captain."

"I know that," you simply answer. "Forgive me for losing my written permission, but I was attacked by rebels not far from here. They stole all my belongings."

"So what is that?" says another soldier pointing at the backpack tied to Thunder's saddle.

"Those are extra clothes and food that I am carrying with me."

"You are a liar," replies the soldier. "You will come with us to our captain."

If you agree to follow the soldiers, walk to section 89

If you resist, run to section 91

91

Quick as the wind, you knock two soldiers unconscious with precise strikes to their temples. A third man rushes at you with a sword, but you easily deflect the weapon and throw the man onto his unconscious companions. The tallest soldier refuses to fight with you, stepping back while taking out a wooden whistle and blowing it.

"He is calling for help! If that noise is the soldiers' alarm, we will soon have company. Let's get out of here, Thunder!"

You jump on your mount and make the horse gallop as fast as it can towards the South. A moment later, you look back and see an army of soldiers chasing you on black horses.

"This is not good. Faster, Thunder! Faster!"

Darkblade's soldiers start shooting arrows at you. You lean forward and ride as low as you can on Thunder's back to avoid being hit.

"The soldiers' arrows have little chance of reaching their target. Keep running Thunder!"

Unexpectedly, your horse falls to the ground and catapults you off its back. With great disgust, you notice a few arrows lodged in Thunder's back legs. You run back to your mount and say:

"Thunder! I'm here for you my friend. I am right here!"

Instinct. You jump high in the air to avoid many arrows coming your way but you suddenly feel a tremendous pain in your right shoulder: a small throwing knife pierced your muscle as you see a yellowish liquid dripping out of your wound. You collapse on the grass, dizzy and weak, the deadly poison working too fast. You and Thunder did you best but for both of you it is...

THE END

92

You leave the unconscious soldier on the filthy ground covered with coal and return to hiding behind the large rock. As you look down at the soldiers, your sharp eyes search for their captain. You look in every direction but cannot find the chief anywhere. As well, you have the weird impression that there are fewer soldiers walking around than before.

"I do not understand," you say to yourself. "The captain was down there a moment ago and is now missing with many soldiers."

The answer to this trivia comes to you too late to try to escape. You quickly turn around and see the captain standing not far behind you next to at least ten other men and women.

"Are you always this noisy when you fight?" asks the captain. "I know who you are, and you are not going anywhere."

The captain then slowly removes the thick red hood and thin mask, exposing a beautiful young woman with long, straight brown hair, and delicate lips.

If you want to defend yourself, jump to section 97

If you wish to surrender for the time being, stand still at section 99

93

You jump onto Thunder's saddle and ride towards the small mountain. As you get closer to it, the burning smell becomes stronger, making breathing more difficult. After riding for a short while, you finally reach the small mountain. You jump to the ground and tell Thunder to wait for you.

The mountain is not very high, and you notice that the ground is covered with a warm coal dust that seems to be carried by the wind from the other side of the mountain. Staying low, you run up the gentle slope towards the nearby top of the mountain to assess the situation.

You reach a large rock and hide behind it to look down at a scene you would never expect to see. At the bottom of the small mountain, you can now see a group of about twenty men and women with red flaming eyes, dressed in red and black uniforms. Each individual immerses huge swords, spears, and other weapons in an enormous pile of red burning coal from which a thick black smoke climbs the sky like a death threat over the world.

"Darkblade's soldiers again!" You whisper to yourself. "They are probably making weapons for their future conquests."

Among the group you notice one individual dressed in an ample red robe with a hood covering the head and some kind of red cloth covering the face up to the eyes. You hear that individual shouting orders to soldiers all around.

"That must be their chief or their captain," you think.

"Hey you!" says a voice behind you. "What are you doing here?"

You turn around and see one of Darkblade's soldiers aiming at you with a crossbow.

If you wish to answer his question, talk to him and go to section 96

If you want to try to neutralize him, fight your way to section 98

94

You tear down the small mountain and reach its bottom where your faithful Thunder is waiting for you. You quickly saddle up and make your horse gallop towards the South as fast as it can, getting away from certain danger.

Continue your journey
to section 95

95

You go on riding towards the South, skirting around the small mountain and wondering when you are going to reach Kholl, the capital of Zaar. You ride for many hours, letting your eyes observe the unknown horizon, and admiring the marvelous beauty. Just before the sunset, you reach a superb plain covered with very long green grass, surrounding a tiny pond with crystal like water. You get off your horse and walk towards the pond. The water looks delicious, and you notice big colorful fish swimming graciously among orange seaweed.

"I think we just found all we need to satisfy our hungry stomachs, don't you think Thunder?"

The splendid animal already drinks the water, swallowing it in huge sips. It then goes on eating the fresh long grass, devouring it with great appetite. Looking at your horse with a smile, you take a sip of water and pull out a small fishing net from your backpack.

"I wonder what those fish taste like."

After catching two big ones and cooking them over a fire, you enjoy a delicious meal while watching the staggering sunset. When the peaceful night finally fills the sky with its shiny stars, you and Thunder quickly fall asleep in the comfortable long grass while listening to the sounds of Mother Nature.

You wake up the next morning at the first sunrays, feeling energized and ready for another exciting day of adventure. Thunder is already awake, eating more grass while staring at you, probably wondering how you can sleep for so long. After saddling up, your white horse starts to gallop once again toward the South, to an imminent and dreadful danger.

Tell Thunder to gallop to section 100

96

You answer the soldier:

"I was on my way back to Kholl when I saw the smoke behind the mountain. I thought somebody's house was on fire, so I came to see if I was right, and if I could help."

"Don't lie to me," replies the man. "You are wearing a rebel's pendent around your neck. I can't remember where I've seen it, but it shows me that you are not as innocent as you claim. Besides, nobody is allowed to live around here, I am sure you know that. Any last wish before you die?"

Hurry to section 98!

97

"I must act know, or I am dead," you say to yourself.

With unbelievable power and speed, you suddenly jump high in the air over the captain, landing behind her, and immediately grabbing her in a solid headlock.

"Step back!" You yell to the soldiers. "Obey and she will live."

"Obey!" ordered the captain. "This lunatic is capable of snapping my neck in a second."

Slowly, the soldiers step back, holding their sword's hilt, ready to launch an attack. Standing behind the young woman and keeping a tight hold around her neck, you yell:

"Let us pass at once!" In an orderly way, Darkblade's soldiers move to your right side, looking hard at you with their red flaming eyes.

"Try anything funny with me, and I promise you will regret it," you tell the captain with a serious voice. Screaming at the soldiers, you then say:

"Try to follow us, and she dies."

Holding your captive firmly, you quickly tumble all the way down the small mountain where Thunder is waiting for your arrival. In a brusque movement, the captain tries to free herself from your hold, but you simply make her pass out with a double finger pressure on her left carotid artery. After putting the woman to the front of the horse, you saddle up and propel Thunder toward the South.

Ride your horse to section 102

98

The soldier presses on the trigger, but the small arrow never reaches you chest. It is caught in mid air by an incredibly fast movement of your hand. Before the man can realize what just happened, you jump into the air, smashing your foot across the soldier's jaw. The man crumbles to the ground, screaming with pain.

If you would like to stay at the top of the small mountain, go to section 92

**If you prefer to leave the mountain,
thinking that you have seen enough, run to section 94**

99

"I surrender," you tell the captain, hoping to have a better chance of escape in a moment.

"That is a wise decision. Put your hands on your head, and stand still."

You obey the captain, but you fall to the ground a split second later, blood spilling out of your abdomen, mixing with the filthy coal. You notice two knives deep in your flesh, provoking an excruciating pain. Your vision becomes blurry, and you understand there is no way back.

THE END

100

You ride the entire day on your faithful animal, wondering when you would reach the capital. You feel exhausted from so many hours of horseback riding, and notice that Thunder is unable to gallop as fast as usual, due to tiredness. Nevertheless, you don't give up, and continue your trek towards the South.

It's already night time when you finally notice a couple of rustic houses in front of you with smoke coming out of their chimneys.

"At last we are in Kholl! It's all thanks to you, Thunder."

The animal answers with a happy neigh, suddenly more energized and picking up speed to reach the houses fast. A moment later, you are officially inside the capital, your horse now trotting on a stone road between the small wooden houses. You immediately notice the delicate and colorful flowers growing in front of each house, perfuming the air with a sweet scent. At the back of each house, you see huge fruit trees growing next to one another in the middle of a wide green garden. A thin smoke comes out of every chimney, coiling up in the sky towards the shiny stars. Every home is built on a big field and has a lot of green space around it.

"This is truly a beautiful place," you tell Thunder. "Everything is so perfect and so well taken care of. There is not one single piece of garbage lying anywhere."

You jump to the ground to stretch your legs, and you walk forward, looking for a place to spend the night. But out of nowhere, you suddenly hear a terrible scream ripping through the air:

"No! Please let us go! We promise it will never happen again. Please! Have mercy!"

If you want to go see where the screams are coming from, hurry to section 103

If you prefer to ignore those screams, thinking it might be a trap, go to section 105

101

You turn your back on the platform and are about to tell Alia and Qelman that you want to leave when a tall man suddenly appears in front of you. He is dressed in a wide white robe, wears a conical hat, and has a thin cloth covering all of his face except his eyes.

"Don't leave now," he tells you. "You can't go to Darkblade's castle now. These people need you."

With amazement you stare at the man and mumble:

"How did you know about my plan?"

"I read your mind," answers the old man, smiling. "Telepathy is a wonderful thing, isn't it? Now go help them, or they will die."

If you wish to listen to the old man, hurry to section 108

If you don't, prepare for section 114

102

After riding for a short while, you notice that Thunder is not galloping as fast as usual. You decide to stop your horse and jump to the ground.

"My poor Thunder. Having an extra weight on your back is a burden, isn't it? Well I think we can fix that."

You pull the unconscious woman off Thunder's back and lay her down on the thick grass. As you look at the captain, an idea suddenly appears in your mind.

"If I wear that red robe, Darkblade's people would think that I am one of their captains," you say out loud. "This could be a huge advantage, but it also could be life threatening."

If you want to take the red robe from the captain, walk to section 104

If you prefer not to take the red robe from the captain and
leave her lying unconscious, saddle up and gallop to section 100

103

You jump onto Thunder's back as the animal starts galloping in the direction of the screams. Between two nearby houses, you see a family of three surrounded by four soldiers dressed in red and black uniforms.

"You did not respect the curfew," says a soldier. "Therefore you have no respect for our master. Follow us to his castle."

"We told you that we were just visiting our neighbors, and that we lost track of time," replies a man holding a little boy by the hand. "We beg you to let us go."

Losing patience, another soldier says: "We are not interested in your excuses, so follow us at once to the castle, or else…"

"Or what?" you brusquely interrupt the soldier.

Your voice has the effect of a bomb whipping everything around it. The soldiers and the family look at you, obviously surprised and dismayed by your sudden appearance.

With a very serious face, you stare at the soldiers and say: "Release them now, or you will have to try to arrest me too."

"That's exactly what we are going to do, stranger," replies a soldier.

Unexpectedly, you jump off Thunder's back, and land just in front of the four soldiers. Before they realize what hit them, you knock them all out with powerful finger strikes to their bodies. The family stands there motionless, staring at you like you are an angel. The mother's boy finds these words to say:

"Thank…thank you so much for saving our lives. Without you…we were doomed. How can we ever repay you?"

"No need," you answer. "It was the least I could do. Just tell me if there is some kind of inn around here."

"Yes there is," says the father's boy, "but Darkblade's guards closed it for the night. As a token of our gratitude, we would like to offer you shelter for the night. Please accept our invitation. You saved our family from a terrible destiny, so let us help you now. We will tie those guards, and hide them in our underground bunker. We will then put your horse in our barn. Would you be our guest?"

If you accept the father's invitation, enter their home at section 107

If you decline the invitation, ride away to section 109

104

Cautiously, you take the captain's robe off. In the outside pockets, you find two throwing knives and a strange golden medallion with a silver rim.

"I wonder what this medallion is used for," you ask yourself, and something tells you that it could be very useful in your mission.

Underneath the robe, the captain is dressed in the red and black uniform worn by Darkblade's soldiers. You look through all the uniform's pockets but do not find anything. While putting the robe in your backpack, you decide to continue your journey without the young woman. You slowly approach her and say:

"Even if you can't hear me, I want you to know that your life was never in jeopardy when you were with me. I have a mission to accomplish, so I had to scare you a little."

As you jump on Thunder's back, the young woman opens her mouth to talk:

"I never asked you to spare me. Do not do me any favours."

"I just did, but I do not expect you to thank me for it," you answer her.

A deep intuition suddenly tells you to continue riding towards the

Southeast. You are fully aware that the capital is toward the South, but that powerful feeling pushes you in a slightly different direction.

**If you want to continue riding toward the South,
ride your horse to section 100**

If you wish to listen to your intuition, make Thunder gallop to section 106

105

"I am sure this is a trap, and I am not going to fall for it," you say out loud. "Let's hurry and find a place to sleep for the night."

You ride away, propelling your horse further towards the South, looking for a secure spot to sleep. A few minutes later, you notice a big hillock covered with grass on your right, close to a tiny forest. You approach the hillock and see a huge opening in it.

"That spot looks cozy enough. Let's stop here, Thunder."

You get down to the ground, and, followed by Thunder, you enter the big hillock. The ground feels rubbery and warm, but all you now care about is sleep. Feeling completely drained, you let yourself roll on the soft ground and quickly fall asleep.

You will wake up in Heaven…or in Hell! During your sleep, some sand creatures appeared from behind a hidden door inside the hillock…and killed you and Thunder while you were both sleeping! It's too bad your mission has to end like this.

THE END

106

Following your intuition, you decide to ride towards the Southeast. After a little while, you reach a small forest near a wide river. You get off your mount to rest and drink some water when a sudden feeling makes you turn around. Behind you, you see an older man floating in the air! The man smiles at you and slowly approaches you, flying above the ground.

"You are *The Chosen One*," the man says. "I have been expecting you for many long years to tell you something very important. The prophecy says that you will save Zaar and the other worlds from Darkblade. Do you think you can accomplish such difficult task?"

"I will try," you simply answer.

"Try not," replies the older man. "Do…or do not! There can be no hesitation in your mind. There will be times when you will doubt yourself, and when you will not know which course of action to take. You must trust your instinct. Trust it at all times! Without it, you are a dead person. I am telling you this so you do not only rely on your special skills and abilities. Remember that the fate of millions of people is in your hands."

"Who are you?" You ask the floating man.

"In time you will find out. You must know one last thing before you go; the magical words to open the doors to Darkblade' secret laboratory are *Ma-Ke-Be-Da-La*. Without those words you will not be able to open the doors, so remember them. Now go, my friend, and be very careful. A long and dangerous journey still lies ahead of you."

You see the man slowly disappear before your eyes. Still amazed by what you just saw and heard, you walk to the river and put some fresh water on your face. After drinking some, you say to Thunder:

"It's a good thing that we came here, right Thunder? I did not think that I could ever meet such a fascinating man almost in the middle of an empty field. I must now remember those magical words for the future."

You drink some more water and say: "Let's go back, Thunder. Kholl is waiting for us."

You jump on your faithful horse, making it gallop towards the South.

Continue your journey to section 100

107

"I accept with pleasure," you answer the father.

The little boy walks up to you and says: "Thank you for not letting them take me away from my mommy and daddy. I was scared."

Squatting in front of the little boy, you tell him: "Nobody is going to take you or your parents away, I promise you that."

Rapidly, you and the parents tie the soldiers and put them into the family's underground bunker behind the house while the little boy brings Thunder inside the barn.

"Nobody will find them in our bunker," says the mother. "Let's keep them there for now." Looking at you with a smile, she says, "I believe it's time to get some rest."

Followed by the family, you enter the house into a wide hallway. The walls are covered with yellowish ceramic tiles, and the floor is made out of big white marble plate. As you step further inside, you walk into a gigantic room furnished with splendid wooden chairs, tables, and leather sofas. The floor is made out of hardwood, and the ceiling is built with thick wood logs. All across the room you notice books and stunning flower bouquets in delicate crystal vases placed on shelves and on small chests of drawers. In the back of the room, a wooden spiral staircase shows the way to the second floor.

"You have a beautiful home," you tell the family. "Where is the kitchen?"

"We don't have one because we don't need one," answers the mother. "We create all our food and basic needs with rudimentary magic."

"And the bathroom?" you ask with a little embarrassment.

"It's at the back of the room to your right," answers the boy with joy in his eyes.

"Are you hungry? You must be," asks the man.

"No thank you. I just need to rest."

"You are welcome to stay here as long as you like," says the woman. "Your room will be the first one upstairs to your right. My son Telik will show you. Have a good night."

The little boy takes your hand and brings you to a gigantic wooden room with a big comfortable bed. After telling him good night, you fall asleep as your head hits the pillow.

Continue your journey to section 110

108

From where you are standing, you jump very high into the air, propelling yourself forward, and landing on the platform, close to the six soldiers. The people of Zaar look at you in disbelief, totally surprised by your sudden appearance. Darkblade's soldiers turn their heads and stare at you then at the ladder, obviously not understanding how you quickly showed up on the platform.

"I will fight you all," you tell the soldiers.

"Are you willing to risk your life to free a bunch of peasants?" asks one of the sorcerer's men.

"You were once yourself a so called "peasant" before being enslaved by Darkblade," you simply answer.

"Nobody among us is a slave," replies another soldier. "And you are about to die."

If you have the skill of ice bolt, run to section 119

If you master the skill of telekinesis, hurry to section 117

If you master the use of the tight web, go to section 115

**If you want to use your magical invisibility skill,
disappear and fight at section 118**

If you have the skill of molecular travel, go to section 116

If you master the skill of telepathy, prepare yourself for section 113

**If you don't have any of the above skills,
or simply do not want to use them, go to section 120**

109

"I don't want to cause you any more trouble," you answer the father's boy. "We can tie and hide those guards together, but for your family's security, I can't stay in your home."

"Please don't go," says the little boy. "You saved us. You are a good person. You didn't do anything wrong."

"Sorry my little friend," you say with a knot in your throat, "but I am sure your parents can later explain this whole situation to you."

Within a couple of minutes, you and the father tie the soldiers and put them into the family's underground bunker. Then, you tell them goodbye after jumping onto your magnificent horse and making it gallop towards the South of the city.

A few minutes later you notice a big hillock covered with grass on your right, close to a tiny forest. You approach the hillock and see a huge opening in it.

"That spot looks good. Let's stop here, Thunder."

You get down to the ground, and, followed by Thunder, you enter the big hillock. The ground feels rubbery and warm, but all you now care about is sleep. Feeling completely drained, you let yourself roll on the soft ground and quickly fall asleep.

You will wake up in Heaven...or in Hell! During your sleep, sand creatures appeared from behind a hidden door inside the hillock...and killed you and Thunder while you were both sleeping! It's too bad your mission has to end like this.

THE END

110

You wake up early the next morning, feeling well rested. After freshening up and putting on your clothes, you walk downstairs to meet your hosts. You see them already sitting at the main table on which wholesome delicacies are laid out.

"Good morning," says the woman. "Did you sleep well?"

"Yes, thank you," you reply.

"Forgive us for skipping the proper introductions yesterday night," she continues. "My name is Alia. This is my husband Qelman, and you know my son Telik."

You slightly bow your head at the family members.

"Please join us at our table," says Qelman. "We are honoured to have you in our house."

"The pleasure is all mine," you tell you hosts. "But you give me too much credit for the help I gave you last night. I am only..."

"My friend," interrupts Alia, "we all know who you are."

"You do?" you ask, perplexed.

"You are *The Chosen One*," says Telik with admiration, sipping on a big glass of strawberry juice.

"Telik is right," continues Alia. "We knew who you were immediately. Who else could have defeated so easily four of Darkblade's guards if not *The Chosen One*?"

"A skilled fighter," you simply answer.

"Women and men from Zaar don't practice fighting arts," adds Alia. "We always lived in peace with one another, and thus never needed to develop such skills. Besides, I am sure that many skilled fighters would have turned their backs on our cries for help, not wanting to waste their time with simple people like us. But you are different. Your heart is pure, and your soul lives to serve others. That is also why you are *The Chosen One*."

"You are too kind," you mumble as your cheeks turn slightly red.

You all sit down, and start eating with great appetite. While savoring the breakfast, your hosts tell you about a very old prophet from Zaar named Dell. Apparently, Dell would be over three hundred years old and would live almost in isolation in a faraway forest. Qelman tells you that about one hundred years ago, when all the people of Zaar were still living in peace, the prophet made a very important announcement to the king. Dell told him that in the near future, a wicked and powerful sorcerer would take over Zaar by force to rule it and would then try to conquer all the other magical worlds. Such news put the king and his entire kingdom in great despair.

Continue your journey to section 111

111

A few days later, Dell found the king again to tell him that he had a dazzling vision. He saw that a certain individual from a completely different world would come to free Zaar and the other magical worlds from the evil dictator and his growing empire. The prophet named this savior *The Chosen One*. Since that day, *The Chosen One* became the ultimate symbol of freedom for the people of all the magical worlds.

"That is a fascinating prophecy," you tell your host.

"And a very real one too," adds Qelman. "Now if you would all excuse me, I have to go lie on the sofa. I have once again one of my famous migraines. I need to rest before we leave to Kholl's main park."

"Why do you wish to go to the main park?" You ask Qelman.

"Today is the day when a team of six guards leaves Darkblade's palace and fly to Kholl's main park. There, they will randomly choose a family and force both parents and children to climb and stand on Darkblade's platform to become his slaves. But…"

"But you know I will not let that happen ever again," you say with a determined voice.

"Thank you for saving all of us," mumbles Telik. "I want to stay with my Mommy and Daddy."

"You will, Telik, I promise you that," you answer the boy. Addressing yourself to Qelman, you say:

"About your migraine, I believe I can help. If you wish, I can try to heal you once and for all."

"Really?"

"I can try," you reply. Qelman nods his head with excitement. You approach him and put your hand on his forehead, feeling the warm healing energy flowing from the centre of your being through your hand, and into the man's head. Alia and Telik look at you with fascination, staring at your hand like at a holy object. After a brief moment, you ask:

"Qelman, how do you feel?"

"This is truly a miracle!" screams the father. "My headache is gone!"

"Gone forever," you add.

"Thank you so much! You relieved me from years of suffering. How can I ever repay you?"

"You can show me the way to the main park and tell me where to find a druid called Keinu," you tell Qelman.

Continue your journey to section 112

112

The man's face becomes white as he says:

"Keinu is a powerful and respected master-wizard who helped people in the entire kingdom. He is now on the run because Darkblade wants to eliminate him. The evil sorcerer feels threatened by Keinu's abilities and knows that the master-wizard will never surrender to him. Unfortunately, nobody knows where Keinu is hiding, but some say he could be in Kholl among us, disguising himself."

"I see," you simply reply. "What about the main park?"

"The main park is located in the centre of Kholl," says Alia. "It used to be a place of serenity and meditation, but now it is a symbol of slavery. The people of Zaar were always very happy with their lives, visiting one another, using magic for their needs, and going for walks in the main park with their families, friends, and pets. Often, the king would organize festivities for all sorts of occasions, and huge crowds would come. As you can see, that was the life everybody here was used to."

"Now," continued Qelman, "people are becoming afraid to walk to the main park, and even to walk down Kholl's streets. Darkblade's guards are constantly patrolling each area, and they could arrest anybody without a reason. As well, the wicked sorcerer threw a spell onto various natural elements of our world, like water and rocks, to create dangerous creatures who obey and idolize him."

"Indeed I already had the pleasure of meeting some of his creatures. I think it is time for us to go and put a stop to all of this, starting with Darkblade's platform," you tell your hosts. "Please show me the way to the main park."

Your hosts get up at once and prepare to leave the house, feeling excited about what will happen in the park with *The Chosen One*. After thanking for their great hospitality, you step outside, followed by the family, and start to walk to the main park.

After about twenty minutes, you all reach the park and walk towards a crowd of people gathered in front of a gigantic wooden platform elevated above the ground. Your heart nearly stops beating when you notice an adorable little girl trembling with fear and crying on the platform next to her parents. In front of them, you see six of Darkblade's soldiers standing with pride, looking down at the crowd.

"People of Zaar," screams a soldier, "who among you will today have the courage to climb the platform and fight the six of us to rescue those poor dogs? Or should we bring these filthy people to our master at once? ANSWER ME!"

If you choose to go on the platform, prepare yourself for section **108**

If you wish to leave to prepare a plan to reach Darkblade's castle,
go to section **101**

113

You close your eyes and can see your six opponents in your mind. You focus on the waves their brains are unconsciously sending and receiving. Those different impulses appear in your mind as water jets flying through the air. Instantaneously, you focus on your own brain waves, which you are perfectly capable of controlling. Then, through a frequency used by the soldiers' brain impulses, you send them the following message:

This is your master Darkblade communicating with you. You must obey the challenger facing you…or die!

"Drop your weapons at once!" You shout at the soldiers. Immediately, Darkblade's loyal servants throw their swords, knives, and bows onto the wooden platform.

"You will fly back to the castle and stay there until further notice," you order them.

Without contesting what you have told them to do, the soldiers peacefully fly away to the castle.

Continue your journey to section 122

114

You turn your back on the old man and go tell Alia and Qelman that you want to leave the main park. They look at you in disbelief, not understanding your motive.

"If you refuse to help those poor people, then I will!" says Alia with fury in her eyes. Before you can say anything, she runs to the ladder, climbs it, and jumps onto the platform.

"I will fight you all," yells Alia towards the soldiers. They all look at her and start to laugh.

"As you wish," says a tall woman with short brown hair, holding a crossbow. "It is your life that is at stake, not ours."

She takes an arrow, arms her weapon, and aims at Alia who stands still on the platform. A second later, the arrow rips through the air…

Fortunately for Alia, the arrow never reaches her heart. In a dazzling reflex, you jump on the platform, and take the hit to protect her. You die instantly, and leave your mission unfinished, but at least you do not die a coward.

THE END

115

In incredibly fast movements, you start creating very precise but strange patterns with your hands as a cloud resembling a fish net appears at the tip of your finger. Without a warning, you throw a large and shiny spider-like net onto the soldiers. As the web lands on them, it immediately closes very tightly, not allowing them to make the slightest movement, almost suffocating Darkblade's men and women.

Continue your journey to section 122

116

You look deeply into your opponents' eyes as they stare at you, pulling out their weapons. Slowly, your body becomes transparent and in the blink of an eye, you completely disappear. Not believing their own eyes, Darkblade's men and women look for you all around them, feeling terrified and vulnerable. They all walk to the spot where you disappeared, some of them bending over and touching the platform. You quickly appear behind them before striking each opponent behind the ear or on the neck with the edge of your hand. The soldiers fall unconscious to the ground, piling up like a bunch of inanimate puppets.

Continue your journey to section 122

117

As the soldiers take out their swords and knives, you notice a pile of big rocks left on the ground next to the platform. In a split second, you look at the rocks before lifting them all up high above the ground with the dazzling power of your mind. Before the six soldiers realize anything, you simply let the big rocks on them! Your opponents crumble onto the platform, bruised and unconscious.

Continue your journey to section 122

118

You start shaking every molecule of your body at tremendous speed as three women soldiers rush at you with long knives. When they are about to reach you, you abruptly disappear. Your opponents suddenly stand still and look all around, feeling petrified by your disappearance. They cannot see you anymore, but you can see them! Immediately, Darkblade's men and women start to drop like flies as you run between them and strike them at the base of their necks. When all soldiers lie unconscious at your feet, you slowly reappear on the wooden platform in front of an amazed crowd.

Continue your journey at section 122

119

You see the soldiers taking out their swords and bows, preparing to attack you. Not intimidated by them, you open a huge flow of magic inside of you. You can now feel the ice coming to the surface of your hands, ready to be used. With amazing dexterity and speed, you throw six gigantic ice bolts towards the soldiers. A moment later, all Darkblade's warriors stand like statues on the platform, completely frozen.

Continue your journey to section 122

120

A massive soldier with very broad shoulders and huge biceps approaches you and says:

"Let's wrestle a little, you and me."

Without adding a word, the big man throws an enormous fist to your face, but you feel the attack before seeing it coming. Sliding to the side, you deflect the fist with your forearm before grabbing the man's uniform with your other hand and throwing him over your shoulder onto the platform. The massive soldier smashes into the wooden boards, breaking them in pieces with his heavy body and pulverizing a thick beam with his head.

Stepping over the now unconscious man, you walk slowly towards the rest of the group. Two women rush at you with their swords, but you jump over them in a dazzling spring, landing in front of the three remaining soldiers, and quickly throwing them off the platform against thick trees. The two-armed women barely have the time to turn around to face you, when you are already on them, applying a quick pressure with your thumbs at the base of their throats, knocking them out, unconscious.

Continue your journey to section 122

121

"Kossol," you tell the horse, "take me to Darkblade's ice palace. Please hurry, because time is not on our side."

With a very loud neigh, the black horse shakes its head as if it is acknowledging your request. Turning its muscular body towards the Southwest, Kossol starts to gallop across the green pastures, picking up speed very quickly.

Within a few seconds, you notice that this magnificent mount is truly as magical as Keinu described it. Kossol develops such an incredible speed that you can hardly see the countryside around you. Suddenly, you feel the animal elevating itself off the ground and galloping on the thin air, reaching the sky extremely fast, and climbing over the tall mountains, the flowing rivers, and the many different villages.

"This horse is just full of surprises," you say to yourself while hanging on to Kossol's reins. "It's a good thing that I am not afraid of heights."

After covering a great distance in the blink of an eye, the black beauty slowly starts to descend from the sky. You notice a scary and shiny structure below, floating on an oval lake: the ice palace! As you get closer to it, you can clearly see the palace's creepy shape: a tremendous ice ball resembling a crystal sphere with at least fifty phenomenally tall and sharp stalagmites surrounding it. As your horse lands on the water, it immediately takes you to the palace's only entrance: a small oval opening carved in the ice ball, just big enough for you to fit through it.

"Wait for me here, Kossol. I don't plan to stay very long in this macabre ice structure."

You enter the palace and find yourself in a narrow corridor enlightened with some kind of blue light. The walls and the ceiling are covered with a thick gray ice, but the floor is surprisingly rough, made out of red pumice stone. You walk through the corridor, which resembles a tunnel, not seeing any doors or entrances anywhere, and not hearing any noises. But at the very end of that corridor, you notice two big ice doors, one in the left wall and the other one in the right wall.

If you want to try to open the left door, walk to section 125

If you wish to try to smuggle yourself through the right door, do it at section 129

If you master the skill of the sixth sense and want to use it, go to section 131

122

It takes a few moments for the people around you to understand what just happened. Suddenly, screams of joy, cheers, and applause break the silence as the family members jump into each other's arms, this time shedding tears of joy and kissing one another.

"That's *The Chosen One*!" yells an old woman from the crowd. "The prophecy was accurate. We are saved!"

The entire crowd suddenly rushes to the platform, cheering for you, clapping their hands, and shouting with happiness as the young father and his wife approach you with their daughter. The man puts his hand on your shoulder, looking straight at you, and says:

"We did not know if the prophecy about *The Chosen One* was true...until now. On behalf of my family, thank you for saving us from a terrible destiny. We will be grateful to you forever."

Staring at you with tears in her eyes, the young man's wife simply takes your hand and smile, not able to find the correct words to express her gratitude. Wanting to thank you as well, the little girl grabs your waist and gives you a hug.

Yelling at the crowd, you say:

"Starting today I recommend that you all avoid this park for the next little while. Until Darkblade is in Zaar, I can't guarantee your protection."

You jump off the platform and approach Alia, Qelam, and Telik who are waiting for you among the crowd, standing speechless after witnessing another one of your great rescues. Out of nowhere, you suddenly hear a delicate whisper in your right ear:

"Don't worry about finding Keinu. He will find you."

You look to your right but see only a crowd of people talking to you and saluting you from everywhere. You quickly leave the park with your new hosts, and run towards their home to get away from all your new admirers. You decide to spend the rest of the day with Qelman and his family, learning about Zaar and about the other great magical worlds while sharing particularities about your own.

At around eight o'clock in the evening, you all hear someone knocking on the door. After opening the door upon Alia's request, you see a tall man standing outside, dressed in a wide white robe, wearing a conical hat with a thin cloth covering all of his face but his eyes.

"You want to find Keinu? Then follow me," says the man.

If you wish to follow the man, walk with him to section 124

If you think it's a trap and refuse to follow him, go to section 126

123

"Kossol," you tell the horse, "take me to Darkblade's labyrinth. Hurry, my friend because we don't have much time."

The black horse shakes its head, acknowledging your request. Turning its strong body towards the West, Kossol starts to gallop across the green pastures, picking up speed very quickly.

Within a few seconds, Kossol develops such an incredible speed that the countryside around you becomes blurry. Suddenly, you feel the animal elevating itself off the ground and galloping on the thin air, reaching the sky extremely fast and climbing over the world.

"Amazing," you say out loud. "This is simply amazing."

After galloping faster than a lightning bolt, the black beauty slowly starts to descend from the sky. A moment later, you find yourself in a scattered forest, at the edge of an artificial desert. You jump off your horse and stare at the horizon. Not too far from your location, you see a truly enormous conic structure elevated on a very thick pile of sand next to a small but deep creek.

"That must be the labyrinth," you say to yourself. "But creeks are not supposed to exist in deserts. This is why Keinu referred to this place as an artificial desert. It is just another one of Darkblade's evil creations."

In front of the labyrinth, you notice many tents pitched in the sand as well as a large group of armed guards keeping an eye on the labyrinth's entrance.

"Wait for me here, Kossol. I will call you when I get back from this creepy place."

Crawling in the sand and hiding behind sand mounds, you slowly approach the labyrinth, constantly staring at your enemies. As you get closer, you can see them in more detail, realizing that the guards are some kind of massive creatures made out of sand, and shaped like humans! Each one of them carries a long bow and a very big sword.

"I must find a way to avoid those sand guards in order to get in."

If you master the invisibility skill, become transparent at section **148**

If you have the fire jet skill, prepare yourself for section **152**

If you don't have any of the above skills, crawl to section **154**

124

You go back to the house to pack your gears, and to say goodbye to the young family.

"We can't thank you enough for saving us from Darkblade' soldiers," says Qelman. "We will be forever grateful."

"And we will pray for you and for your mission' success," continues Alia." As she says those words, Telik runs to you and hugs you.

"Thank you for your hospitality," you tell the family. "Zaar will be saved, I promise you. I have a strong feeling that I must continue my journey without Thunder, so please take good care of my loyal horse."

You walk outside and without saying a word, you follow the mysterious man dressed in white. Together, you walk on the stone road through the center of Kholl, between the small wooden houses. As the night slowly falls on the capital, you notice very few people passing by, fleeing into their homes, fearing Darkblade's people. Suddenly, the dark sky seems like a fearful menace hanging over the world, making the moon resemble to a macabre ghost's face.

Brusquely, the man dressed in white turns around and puts his hand on your head. Immediately, you feel sucked into a powerful whirlwind as your entire being starts spinning in it. You have the impression that all your body's molecules are detaching themselves from one another, yet staying close together while traveling at tremendous speed through a great distance.

The spinning suddenly stops as you find yourself in a very large room lightened by at least one thousand candles sticking out of the yellowish rubber walls and high ceiling. All around you, you notice rows of shelves inlaid in the walls and a very large blue octagonal table made out of marble, placed in the middle of the room. Neatly placed on every shelf, you see all sorts of old books, triangular mugs, short plants, powders in transparent containers, liquids in crystal jars, and weird metal instruments. In front of you stands the man dressed in white, looking calmly at you.

"Welcome to my hideout," says the man, smiling. "My name is Keinu."

Continue your journey to section 127

125

You push against the left door and see a sight you would have never expected. In front of you, a stunning white beach bordering a marvelous turquoise sea takes your breath away. Birds are flying across the clear blue sky as tiny colorful fish jump in and out of the water.

"I just found a small paradise. What a beauty!"

As you say those words, you walk through the door. You barely have the time to put a foot on the beach before its sand brusquely turns into red pumice stone, everything around you transforming into ice. It is too late to understand that you have fallen into a deadly trap. From the high icy ceiling, a sharp stalactite falls directly onto your head, killing you instantly. First appearances are not always right, but that does not matter to you anymore because your life and mission just ended.

THE END

126

"I will not follow you anywhere," you tell the mysterious man dressed in white. "I have no proof that you are not one of Darkblade's agents, or that you are not some kind of assassin. Leave immediately and never come back here if you know what is good for you."

"The High Priest from Tibet sends me. He told me that you must meet Keinu," the man replies slowly.

You suddenly feel blood rushing through your veins as your heartbeat accelerates.

"If this man knows the High Priest from Tibet and is therefore aware of my world, then he must be telling the truth," you think to yourself. "I don't

believe Darkblade himself nor any one of his people have ever heard of the High Priest, nor of a place called *Tibet*."

"You are absolutely correct," says the man dressed in white. "Isn't telepathy a wonderful thing?"

Smiling at him, you say:

"I apologize for doubting you. I wasn't sure who you were at first. I will follow you to Keinu."

Continue your journey to section 124

127

Taking off the mask he uses as a camouflage, Keinu says:

"Forgive me for not introducing myself sooner. I was afraid you wouldn't believe me."

"Where are we?" you ask.

"You are in one of my many hideouts. This one is located to the North of Kholl, in a small cave. I brought you here to help you accomplish your mission. But to do so, you must help me first."

"How did you find out that I am who the people of Zaar call *The Chosen One*?"

"The High Priest from Tibet and I are close friends. Telepathically, he sent me a mental picture of you, telling me you are *The Chosen One*."

"You said I must help you in order for you to help me. To what were you referring?" you ask, perplexed.

"A while ago, Darkblade started to build his army by creating all sorts of living creatures loyal to him. He ordered them to arrest me, feeling threatened by my abilities. Since that day I have disguised myself, staying in my many hideouts and awaiting your arrival."

Keinu stops talking for a moment before recalling a sad incident.

"One evening, the sorcerer's creatures forced their way into my main laboratory in Kholl. They did not find me and destroyed everything, killing all my six wing birds. Darkblade ordered his creatures to steal two very important items from me so he could eventually use them to increase his own magical abilities. Since that day the wicked master of black magic told his monsters to guard the belongings he stole from me in secret hideouts of which I know the whereabouts. In order for me to help you, you must bring back my belongings so I can prepare the magical potion to erase a part of Darkblade's memory. Without those items, I cannot prepare the potion, and thus you cannot complete your mission."

"I see. Where do I have to go, and what do I have to bring back?"

"You must reach two different secret hideouts. One is a monstrous ice palace magically built by the sorcerer, located to the Southwest of Kholl and floating on an oval lake. You will have to enter the deadly palace, find my magic book of spells, and bring it back here to me."

"What about the second hideout?"

"The second one is a gigantic conic labyrinth in the middle of an artificial desert. It's located to the West of Kholl, and your quest is to bring back my silver powder of memory. We are running out of time, so you must hurry."

Continue your journey to section 128

128

"Is there anything specific you can tell me about those two hideouts?"

"You must know that those places are extremely dangerous. There are traps almost everywhere, with immoral creatures slaying all uninvited visitors. The curious ones who reached and entered the hideouts never made it back. Make sure you do."

"I will," you answer with a flame of determination in your eyes.

"If you know how to fly, refrain from it. You would bring too much attention to yourself and would therefore become more vulnerable to your enemies. As you are also aware, not having a clear picture of the hideouts in your mind makes it impossible for you to fly at the speed of mind. Without an exact mental image of the locations you want to reach at such unimaginable speed, you would not know when to precisely stop flying, and thus could never find these secret places."

"Thank you for your advice, Keinu."

The master-wizard walks up to the octagonal table and pushes on a red porcelain sphere inlaid in the blue marble. Automatically, a secret door opens in the right wall. Behind the door, you see a breathtaking forest with strange but adorable animals, looking like tiny balls of fur, playing with one another. But most of all, you notice a splendid black horse feeding on wild berries.

"Meet Kossol, my magical horse," says Keinu. "You tell it where you want to go, and it will bring you there…in no time!" Putting his hand on your shoulder, Keinu says:

"Now go, my friend, and come back to me alive."

You salute the master-wizard, and step outside into the wonderful, thick forest. Immediately, Kossol comes to you and starts to lick your hand. Grabbing its saddle, you jump onto your new mount, ready to face your dreadful and deadly quests.

If you wish to reach the icy palace, saddle up to section 121

If you choose to find the labyrinth, ride to section 123

129

Feeling the ice almost freezing your palms, you put your two hands against the right door and start pushing against it. Without squeaking, the door opens up to a large icy and triangular room, also enlightened with some kind of blue light. Exactly like in the corridor you have just been in, the room's walls and its ceiling are covered with a thick gray ice, but the floor is made out of red pumice stone. You enter the perfectly symmetric room, feeling the cold air rubbing your skin.

"This room is completely empty. There is nothing but ice, pumice stone, and that strange blue light glowing out of nowhere. I really wonder where the light is coming from."

As you say those words, you notice three doors in the wall to your left. One is gray like the room's ice, one is tall and white, and the last one is black and wide. You walk towards the doors, wondering which way to go.

If you wish to open the white door, walk to section 130

If you prefer opening the black door, push against it at section 132

If you want to open the gray door, go to section 134

If you have the sixth sense skill, focus to section 136

130

You choose to open the white door. Behind it, there is an ice wall with a circular entrance carved in it. As you approach the entrance, you notice that it is some kind of very long and narrow tunnel enlightened with the same blue artificial light. You enter the tunnel head first and realize that you must crawl to be able to go forward.

After crawling for a while, the tunnel brusquely becomes a very slippery slope, and you start to slide down.

"This is amusing! I always loved slides."

But after sliding for an hour, and then for the entire day, you understand that you have fallen into a deadly trap. You try to stop sliding, doing everything in your power, but you cannot! You will continue sliding for a month, for a year, for a decade…forever! But do not worry, you will be dead by then. You have fallen into a magical trap cursed by Darkblade in which you will slide for eternity without being able to stop. You will die of thirst and hunger, so you will only be stuck here for about a week before being completely dehydrated. It is too bad that your mission has to end now when you were so close to completing it!

THE END

131

As you approach the doors, your sixth sense urges you not to open the left one. You feel an imminent danger on the other side of it, threatening your life, like a wild beast waiting for you to show up to jump on you and rip you apart. Between life and death, you choose life.

Continue your journey to section 129

132

You open the black door, and behind it you see a narrow vertical tunnel with a steel ladder embedded into its wall. The ladder seems to join the room you are in to another one above you. You start climbing the short ladder, and quickly come out of the vertical tunnel, finding yourself in a room looking exactly like the one below. You walk around the empty room, looking for some kind of door, but you do not see any. You touch the icy walls and the floor made out of red pumice stone, hoping to find a hidden exit, but you find nothing.

"This is just a dead end," you say, staring at the shiny walls made out of ice. Suddenly, you notice that the wall across the ladder you just climbed seems to start moving, almost like water at the surface of a pond. You approach the wall, and you spontaneously reach out with your hand to touch it…but your hand goes right through it!

"A wall made out of water…and it's not even dripping! How is that possible? Maybe I am facing some kind of secret door."

If you wish to try to go through the watery wall, jump to section 137

If you want to go back down and try to open the gray door,
walk down to section 134

133

From behind the small mountain familiar silhouettes appear. An army of muscular men and women carrying bows and other weapons wave at you with smiles on their faces. Among them, you recognize a very old man sitting on a stunning white horse.

"Dunlop the wise chief!"

You wave to your friends as they run down the gentle slope. You welcome them with open arms as they quickly surround you and greet you warmly.

"My friends!" you scream with joy. "What an incredible surprise! What are you doing hanging around this dangerous place, and how did you know I was here?"

The wise chief approaches you on his beautiful white mount and tells you:

"Knowing well this area, we all figured that you would eventually stumble over this small mountain, and meet an army of Darkblade's soldiers. We decided to come over here and see if we could be of any help." Looking at you with his deep eyes, Dunlop starts laughing before saying: "We saw the way in which you neutralized your opponents, and now we are not so sure if you need our help at all!"

"Your help is always greatly appreciated, but you don't have to put your lives at stakes."

"It is the least we could do to help *The Chosen One*," continues Dunlop. "The other reason we came is to give you my best horse *Thunder*. I know you want me to keep my best mount, but I must insist for you to take it. To successfully complete your mission, you will sometimes have to avoid flying to keep your enemies away. That's why you definitively need a horse…and the best one!"

"In this case, I accept your mount," you tell Dunlop. "Thank you very much to all of you for helping me out. A person is always in need of good friends." Looking at the old wise man, you say: "Don't worry. I will take great care of this superb animal."

"I have no doubt that you will. Good luck to you my friend," says Dunlop. "We will pray for your success and to see you back alive."

Petting your new companion *Thunder*, you wave to your friends as they return to their hideout, promising yourself not to let them down.

Continue your journey to section 135

134

You easily open the gray door by pushing on it with your hands. To your surprise, the door opens to a large, rectangular icy closet. The closet is empty and covered with ice, but you immediately notice a yellow slide embedded in the floor. It slopes downward, going underneath the floor, and it is made out of an extremely slippery ice.

"I wonder where this slide is leading to. Let's find out."

Get ready for section 143

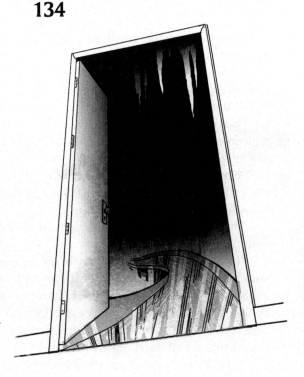

135

Leaving the captain lying on the ground, you jump onto Thunder's saddle, ready to ride towards the South. Suddenly, the young woman looks at you and says:

"Don't leave me in pain lying like this. Kill me first, and then leave."

"Sorry, lady," you answer, "but I have no intention of killing you. Every life form deserves to be preserved. Remember that, because your master Darkblade obviously taught you the wrong lesson."

She simply stares at you, not understanding the meaning of your words. You then simply add:

"In time you will understand the essence of what I just said. Today, I am letting you live, so you should do the same for others."

You propel your strong mount towards the South, feeling more and more the heavy responsibility of succeeding in your mission.

Continue your journey to section 100

136

Using your sixth sense, you try to feel which way to go...but you cannot anymore! Even after focusing on the energy within yourself and on your mental powers, you are still unable to pinpoint the direction you must follow. It is as if someone or something annihilated your ability to use your sixth sense.

"This is very strange," you say out loud. "I don't know what is happening to me, but I hope it's only temporary."

As you say those words, you remember what someone told you not long ago: "Trust your instincts at all time." Staring at the three doors, you think that it is probably the best advice you could follow to stay alive.

"So which way should I go?"

If you wish to open the white door, walk to section 130

If you prefer opening the black door, push against it at section 132

If you want to open the gray door, go to section 134

137

Head first, you jump towards the watery wall. Your body goes right through the wall, and you let yourself roll on the other side of it, now finding yourself in a narrow corridor.

"This corridor looks exactly like the one I entered when I penetrated inside the ice palace, but I don't see any doors or exits anywhere."

As you say those words, you start walking forward, staring at the icy walls around you, observing the strange red pumice stone, and still wondering where the omnipresent blue light comes from. You walk for about ten minutes before reaching a white icy wall blocking your way.

"This is a dead end. There is nothing here to see but a white wall made out of ice. I guess I have to go back to the watery wall."

Disappointed, you turn around to walk back, but a sudden noise makes you stop. Behind you, the white icy wall moves. You approach it slowly, ready to defend your life. Without any other warning, the white wall abruptly explodes like a grenade, sending you flying across the corridor. You hit the floor without any damage, but you notice tiny ice palates planted in your chest, face, and legs.

"Those palates are not planted very deep," you say out loud. "They should melt in no time. At least the white wall is gone, and I can keep going forward."

"Not so fast", says a deep voice in front of you. "You are going to have to go through us first!"

Behind the ice debris left by the explosion, you notice three gigantic forms walking your way. A moment later, you realize that you are facing three enormous ice monsters. Each one is twice your height, has four legs as big as steamrollers, four arms thick like tree trunks, and fists bigger than huge pumpkins. You notice that each monster is holding a very long and sharp stalagmite.

"This is not good..."

If you wish to run away, propel yourself to section 139

If you master the fire jet skill, don't waste any time and go to section 140

If you want to fight the three monsters but do not have the fire jet skill,
fight for your life at section 142

138

You walk forward, not seeing any doors on either side of the corridor, until you reach the end of it.

"This time, I really think that I hit a dead end."

You touch the icy wall in front of you to make sure it is not a watery wall hiding a secret passage. To your great disappointment, the wall's ice is hard as a brick.

"That's what I thought," you say to yourself. "Let's go back to try to find another passage. I must find that magical book of spells."

You are about to go back when a delicate sliding noise makes you abruptly turn around. You look at the floor behind you and see two old pumice stone plates sliding to the side. Under the plates, you notice two long and wide slides that seem to be sloping downwards. Each slide is made out of an extremely slippery ice, but the left one is green, and the right one is yellow.

"Something tells me that I just found some very interesting passages."

If you wish to slide down the green slide, prepare yourself for section 141

If you want to slide down the yellow slide, slide to section 143

139

You turn your back to your three enemies and start running as fast as you can in the opposite direction.

"I have to reach the watery wall. My life depends on it!"

A brusque and atrocious pain pins you to the floor, making you look down at your pectoral muscles. With horror, you realize that two sharp stalagmites are coming out of your chest.

"Those creatures threw those stalagmites at me," you mumble with less and less strength. "I should have known better than to try to run away."

When the ice monsters reach you, you are already dead, lying in your blood and mucus. Running away from your predators was not a success this time, but that does not matter now because you are gone for good. You will be missed by all, even if Zaar and the other magical worlds are doomed and will now suffer…forever!

THE END

140

You stare at the three gigantic ice monsters, focusing on the thick ice covering their large bodies while opening a huge flow of magic inside of you. You feel the fire coming to the surface of your hands, making them hot and steamy and almost burning them. Without any warning, an impressive fire jet comes out of your hands and crashes into the huge creatures, melting them in seconds! The ice monsters become smaller and smaller, looking like some kind of weird ice sculptures disappearing in the hot sun. They quickly turn into a large puddle of water covering the red pumice stone, the transparent liquid now resembling a puddle of dirty blood.

Shaking your steamy hands, you stride over the water and ice debris before resuming your walk forward.

Continue your journey to section 138

141

You sit at the top of the green slide and let yourself slide down. You find yourself in a very large and wide tunnel, strongly lightened by the same blue artificial light. The tunnel's slope is very gentle and straight, so you don't develop much speed. After only a short while, your feet suddenly hit an ice wall as you stop sliding down.

"This is the end of the tunnel? Where is the exit?"

Instinctively, you smash your heel into the wall. Under the powerful blow, the ice suddenly breaks, leaving you no other choice than to free-fall! Fortunately, your fall is a very short one, and you land safely on a hard floor made out of red pumice stone. You look around and notice that you are in a small empty room. In one of the walls, you see four tunnels carved in the ice.

"How strange. The ice in each tunnel has a different color. It's either orange, brown, silver, or gold. I guess I have to choose where I want to go from here!"

If you want to go into the orange tunnel, walk to section 145

If you wish to try your luck going into the brown tunnel, run to section 147

If you prefer entering the silver tunnel, propel yourself to section 149

If you choose to walk into the gold tunnel, get ready for section 151

142

Staring at you as if you were a tiny bug, one of the three ice monsters says:

"I am going to break you, and then squash you!"

The creature swings the long and sharp stalagmite at your legs, but you avoid the hit by jumping high over the weapon and forward. At the same time, you smash your heel into the monster's head, breaking it into small pieces and catapulting the giant backwards. Stunned by what you just did, the two other creatures carefully approach you side by side, each holding a stalagmite with four hands. Unexpectedly, you run toward the two monsters and stop right between them, as if you were waiting to get hit across the head or ripped apart.

In a terrible roar, one of the giants swings his weapon above his head twice before suddenly trying to hit your skull to crack it open. As you quickly tilt your head forward to avoid the extremely powerful blow, you hear something like an extraordinary ice explosion right behind you. You turn around and see the third ice creature crumbling to the floor. If you avoided the amazingly powerful blow, its head certainly did not!

"Thanks for doing the job for me," you tell the ice monster facing you. As you say those words, you pulverize its waste with a fantastic elbow strike, turning the giant into a pile of ice.

Continue your journey to section 138

143

You sit at the top of the yellow slide and let yourself slide down. You find yourself in a very small and narrow tunnel, barely lightened by the same blue artificial light. You have to lie down to avoid rubbing your head against the upper part of the small tunnel. Quickly, you develop an impressive speed in this crazy tunnel built with very tight turns, large loops, and long spirals.

"I feel like I am in a dangerous roller-coaster!"

After sliding for at least ten minutes, you lift your head a little and notice a very bright light coming through a big hole ahead of you. You realize that the tunnel you are in will soon go through that hole.

"Is the tunnel continuing beyond that hole, or…?"

You don't have the time to finish your thought. As you slide through the asymmetric hole carved in the icy wall, a horrific feeling seizes you when you realize that the tunnel has been cut off! Before you know it, you find yourself outside the ice palace, flying through the air and falling very fast. Luckily for you, the speed you developed in the tunnel also catapulted you away from the palace, helping you dive straight into the oval lake!

After coming back to the lake's surface, you scream with joy "I'm alive! I'm alive!" Catching your breath, you tell yourself that you must get out of this lake before I freeze to death.

You swim to shore and pull yourself out of the freezing water. Your horse Thunder looks at you, very surprised of your sudden appearance.

"I guess I have to start this quest all over again. In addition to this, I don't have any extra clothes", you tell the animal. "Wait for me here."

You run back to the ice palace and go through the entrance. You find yourself again in a narrow corridor enlightened with the blue light. You walk through the narrow corridor until you reach its very end. There, you notice once again two big ice doors: one in the left wall, and the other one in the right.

If you want to try to open the left door, walk to section 125

If you wish to try to smuggle yourself through the right door, do it at section 129

If you master the skill of the sixth sense and want to use it, go to section 131

144

With great agility, you jump over the wooden table and almost land on top of the druid, smashing your foot into his chest. The old man falls flat on his back and panics, not able to breathe at all. You turn around to grab the book...but it disappeared! Behind you, you hear a whistling voice saying:

"Is this what you want, stranger?"

With great disgust, you see one of the carnivorous plants looking straight at you with yellow sparkling eyes, holding the magical book of spells on one of its long green stems, which looks more like a deadly tentacle. The plant smiles at you and says:

"If you want this book so badly, why didn't you just ask for it? It makes things so much easier."

To your astonishment, the plant throws the book at your feet, still smiling.

"It's now or never," you tell yourself.

You dive forward to get the book, but before you can reach it, a powerful stem wraps around your waist and lifts you high above the floor, suffocating you. You feel the stem slowly entering your skin, and before you can defend yourself using your magic, you are transformed into a human yo-yo, your head smashing the floor every time. Blood pours down your face as you see your opponents getting closer to you. You barely have the time to see the old druid gesturing at you when an amazing electric current hits you like a ton of bricks...and makes your heart stop. That's it for you. You did your best.

THE END

145

You walk into the orange tunnel. After taking a couple of steps, a smell of fresh oranges hits your nostrils.

"Well this is very nice!" you say out loud. "I guess I chose the right tunnel!"

You barely finish saying those words when four gigantic ice monsters abruptly appear in front of you. Immediately, you pulverize two of them with punches to their huge chests, but a tremendous stalagmite hits you across the head, and you fall unconscious to the ground.

You wake up in Darkblade's palace about two hours later, chained to a very thick brick wall. In a moment, you will finally meet the evil sorcerer. He will pronounce a magical formula while forcing you to look at him straight in his eyes, and you will become his most dangerous and loyal assassin. Your mission is over, and now millions of people will suffer… because of you!

THE END

146

Fast as lightning, you launch forward and grab the old book before anyone or anything can stop you. As you turn around to escape, you notice a couple of low windows at the back of the room. In front of those windows, you see tiny plants sunbathing.

"If those plants are getting sun from outside, it means I can exit this palace through those windows! It's my only chance."

"Kill the stranger and get the book back!" shouts the druid behind you.

You start running across the gigantic room, avoiding the huge monsters and the carnivorous plants. In a matter of seconds, big stalagmites, lightning bolts, and poisonous sprays are thrown in your direction, but your deep survival instinct makes you roll onto the floor, jump into the air, and dive forward to avoid being hit. You are about to reach one of the windows when a thin tentacle wraps around your wrist, pulling you backwards. Instinctively, you bring your wrist to your mouth and bite off the tentacle. A nasty liquid suddenly fills your mouth as an ice monster grabs you from behind. You turn around and spit the liquid in the creature's face, instantaneously melting its entire head and burning your mouth.

"Don't let the intruder get away!"

In an ultimate effort, you launch toward one of the primitive windows carved in the icy wall and jump through it, breaking its thin glass. Flying across the air, you hit one of the fifty stalagmites surrounding the ice palace. Immediately and at great speed, you start sliding down the tremendous and sharp ice pole, realizing that you are not too far from the ground. You quickly land in a big pile of snow and start running forward.

"Kossol!" you yell at the top of your lungs. "I am here!"

Right away, the magnificent horse appears from behind one of the stalagmites, and greets you by licking your hand. Jumping on its back, you tell the animal:

"Get us back to your master Keinu. Our quest here is finished."

With a very loud neigh, the beautiful black mount starts galloping on the thick snow, propelling itself high into the air, and disappearing with you across the blue sky.

**If this quest is the first one you finished,
continue your journey to section 150**

If you have completed both quests, hurry to section 160

147

You choose to go into the brown tunnel. You walk forward for almost two hours without seeing anything else but the brown ice covering the walls.

"This tunnel must end somewhere. I just hope that I am not going to fall into some nasty trap."

After a short while, you hear a voice coming from behind a certain part of the left wall. You stop and put your head against the wall, trying to hear every word.

"Now it says that I must add some purple egg shell powder to the formula," says a voice.

You stay close to the wall to get more information, pressing against it with your ear and palms. In an unexpected movement, the wall abruptly slides to the side, sending you forward on your stomach. You jump back on your feet, and notice at least one hundred gigantic ice monsters staring at you from every corner of a huge room filled with tall plants feeding on some kind of meat! To your right, you lay your eyes on an old man, probably a druid, making some kind of gray smoky potion on a very long wooden table covered with all kinds of glass jars, roots, powders, liquids, and all sorts of strange accessories. Not too far from the old man, you notice an old open book lying on the wooden table.

"Protect the magical book of spells at all costs!" yells the druid. "Kill the intruder!"

As he screams those words, the old man starts running towards the book.

If you wish to neutralize the old druid, jump to section 144

If you prefer trying to take the book and escape, run to section 146

148

You look at the sand guards while focusing on accelerating the movement of your body's molecules. Slowly, your skin becomes transparent, and a few seconds later, you become completely invisible. You get up and walk normally towards the labyrinth's entrance, not worrying about your footprints left in the sand because of the constant wind blowing on its surface, erasing every trace. Without any incidents, you easily pass the sand guards and step into the gigantic conic structure.

Continue your journey to section 153

149

You enter the silver tunnel and walk straight ahead. After a short while, you notice that the artificial and omnipresent blue light is getting weaker and weaker. You look around and say:

"Where does that light come from? It must be…"

You do not have the chance to finish your sentence. Unexpectedly, the floor collapses, and you have nowhere else to go but down. You fall into a complete darkness, feeling cold and scared, exactly like during your plane accident nine years ago. The only difference is that this time there is no way out for you. You see, Darkblade has created a horrific and deadly monster to greet you in a place where you have never been before. To say the least, in about ten seconds, you will find yourself in the huge mouth of giant piranha with extremely sharp teeth. Now you imagine the rest…

THE END

150

In no time, you are back at Keinu's hideout. The master-wizard greets you with open arms, happy to see you and Kossol alive.

"I knew that you would succeed," says the man as you give him back his precious item. "I can't imagine how difficult it must have been to complete this quest."

"It was quite an adventure," you tell the old man.

Putting his hand on your shoulder, the master-wizard smiles and says:

"Thank you so much. I truly appreciate your help."

Giving you a big plate of delicious food, the wizard goes on saying:

"I believe you and Kossol both deserve to fill up your stomachs and get a good night's sleep before leaving for your next quest tomorrow morning."

"That is a great idea," you answer with a smile.

After eating with the wizard and telling him everything that happened, you wish him good night and let yourself fall on a bed made out of compacted soft grass in some kind of duvet cover.

Keinu gently wakes you up the next morning before inviting you to join him for a delightful breakfast. Once again, you eat with great appetite, feeling very energized and ready to fulfill your next quest.

"Your next quest might be even more difficult than the first one," says Keinu. "Remember to trust your instincts and to use your magical skills wisely. I will be waiting for your return."

Followed by the master-wizard, you step outside the hideout to find Kossol. Proud of riding such an extraordinary horse, you pet the animal before jumping on its back.

"Are you ready for our next quest, Kossol?"

The horse answers you with a very loud neigh. Looking then at Keinu, you say:

"I will be back soon, I promise."

"I know you will," answers the old man. "You take care of yourself, my friend. I will be waiting for you. I wish you all the luck and protection in the world."

You smile at the wizard and propel your mount forward towards a new dangerous adventure.

If you want to reach the icy palace, saddle up to section 121

If you must find the labyrinth, ride to section 123

151

Carefully, you step into the gold tunnel. After taking about ten steps, the tunnel abruptly turns to the left, and to your surprise, you find yourself in an extremely large room with a very big window. The walls, the ceiling, and the floor seem to be made out of gold, but what truly catches your attention is what stands in the middle of the room: a small golden table with an old dusty book placed on top of it.

"The magical book of spells! I finally found it!"

You are about to enter the golden room when your instinct suddenly tells you to stop.

"I am sure this room is full of traps. Let's not rush into anything, and let's be very careful."

Looking all around you, you enter the room, walking very carefully. As you slowly reach the table, you notice holes inside the walls and sharp blades fixed to the ceiling.

"I am almost there."

Getting closer and closer, you quickly glance at the cover of the book lying on the table…and it is not what you were expecting! A dreadful feeling grabs you by the throat as you read the book cover: *Darkblade is expecting you…right here…right now!*. You stare at the book as it suddenly turns into flames.

"I must get out of here fast!"

In a dazzling spring, you jump high into the air and avoid a thousand poisoned arrows flying out of the walls. You then slide under the golden table to avoid being sliced by all the blades falling from the ceiling.

"RAAAAAH! RAAAAAH!"

You look towards the window and suddenly see five gigantic ice birds with very long and nasty beaks flying in. As fast as you can, you start running towards the tunnel's entrance, but a staggering pain stops you…dead! Thin long spears suddenly come out of the floor, piercing every part of your body right through. You were very close to completing this quest and your mission, but unfortunately, for you it is now…

THE END

152

"I must distract them in some way," you say to yourself.

You stare at a nearby creek, focusing on its clear water while opening a huge flow of magic inside of you. In a quick movement, a very long fire jet comes out of your hands and crashes into the water, making an amazing splash! But to your great surprise, you suddenly hear:

"The fire jet came from over there. Let's check it out!"

Immediately, you see a bunch of massive guards running in your direction. They are about to reach you when you suddenly get off your stomach, and jump over them, aiming for the labyrinth's entrance.

"Intruder alert! Shoot the arrows now!!"

Suddenly, the unexpected happens as one of your legs gets stuck in some vicious quicksand. You try to get out of it, but the more you move, the more you are sucked in. Desperately, you try to free yourself in any way possible, but it's in vain. Soon, the quicksand will swallow your entire body...to the sand guards' delight! It's too bad that your mission has to end this way.

THE END

153

You find yourself in a wide tunnel, facing a thick staircase made out of stone. The walls and the floor are built with huge blocks of stone. As for the ceiling, it is constructed with thin stone plates laid out and solidified one next to another. You run up the stairs and reach the top very fast. You find yourself at the beginning of a very large but short hallway at the end of which a massive stone wall has been built. In that wall, you see four large stone doors. Curiously, a different animal has been painted in red on every door.

Trust your instincts and your intuitions. If you do, you will always find the right path.

You always remembered those words said to you years ago by the High Priest of Tibet. Now they echo in your head once again. You stare at the four heavy doors, trying to feel which one to open.

Our destiny is in your hands.

If you wish to open the door with the bear, walk to section 155

If you choose to open the door with the snake, open it at section 157

If you prefer to open the door with the tiger, hurry to section 159

**If you want to open the door with the monkey,
prepare yourself for section 161**

154

Carefully, you keep crawling while hiding behind sand mounds. Your objective is to first reach the back of the conic structure, and eventually enter it from the front.

"I hope that the back of the labyrinth is less guarded than the main entrance."

After crawling for a very long time, you can finally see the back of the gigantic structure from a secure distance. You smile when you notice only three sand guards standing there.

"I will wait for the night to fall before taking care of those guards. I can't take the risk of being seen now."

Lurking in the sand, you patiently wait many hours for the dark night to appear, studying your enemies' every move. You then start crawling again towards the back of the conic structure, your eyes staring at the three guards. As you get closer, you hear one of them say: "I will see you in the morning."

The sandman leaves and disappears inside a tent. With only two guards remaining, you smile at the fact that your task just became easier. Like a tiger measuring the distance between itself and its prey, you stay low in the sand, waiting for the perfect moment to attack. Without making a sound, you brusquely propel yourself onto the guards and pulverize their forehead with your fists. The massive sandmen don't have the time to realize what hit them and simply collapse in the sand, their heads turned into dust. Cautiously, you then crawl behind a nearby tent to take a look at the entrance.

"There are now only five creatures guarding the entrance! The rest of them probably went to sleep. I will have to act extremely quickly and silently."

Very slowly, you crawl towards the main entrance, keeping your eyes on the sand creatures. You can hear them whisper among themselves, talking about irrelevant things. As they take a couple of steps forward, you subtly sneak behind them. With five extremely powerful and precise blows, you strike them all at the base of their necks with the edge of your hands, turning them partly into a pile of filthy sand. Without wasting any more time, you walk toward the entrance and step inside the enormous conic structure.

Continue your journey to section 153

155

You stare at the door on which a huge red bear is painted, and decide to open it. You step into a small room entirely built out of gray stone plate, and notice that it is full of dead bears stuffed with straw. All the species are displayed, either hanging on the walls or placed on the stone floor.

"Why would someone kill all those beautiful animals?" you ask yourself.

In the left corner of the room, behind a very tall grizzly bear, you notice two doors. On each one, two different animals are painted in red. There is a polar bear on the left door, and a lion on the right one.

If you want to open the left door, go to section 156

If you prefer opening the right door, walk to section 158

156

After opening the door with a polar bear painted on it, you find yourself in a huge circular room, its floor being the bottom of a very tall conic tower. Immediately, you lay your eyes on a solid staircase built with heavy stones, placed in the middle of the room. Without wasting any time, you start climbing the staircase spiraling upwards, hoping to be on the correct path.

After climbing the stairs for almost an hour, you finally reach the top of the conic tower. You heart palpitates as you notice two heavy closed doors in front of you. Suddenly, a strong artificial blue light enlightens the top of the tower. Straightaway, you feel mentally weaker and unsure about what your instinct is telling you. You sit down for a moment, trying to free yourself from that unpleasant feeling.

"This light has some kind of strange power over me. Since it started to glow all around me, I can't hear my deep inner voice telling me what to do."

You stare at the two wooden doors, realizing that opening either one of them could mean life…or death.

If you choose to open the left door, jump to section 167

If you prefer trying your luck with the right door, walk to section 169

157

You open the door with a snake painted on it. You step in a small room where the walls, ceiling, and floor are built with stone plates. You notice that the room is full of dead snakes stuffed with straw. All the species are displayed, and are hooked on the walls or placed in glass jars.

"This is all wrong," you say out loud.

In the right corner of the room, behind a very large boa constrictor, you notice two doors. On each one, two different animals are painted in red. There is a buffalo on the left door, and a jaguar on the right one.

If you want to open the left door, go to section 162

If you prefer opening the right door, walk to section 164

158

After opening the door with a lion on it, you step into a room looking exactly like the previous one but quite a bit larger, and you see a tremendous elephant stuffed with straw sitting on the stone floor.

"What is it with all those stuffed animals?" you ask yourself.

There is nothing other than the elephant in that large room. To your surprise, a strong elephant smell fills the room, as if the big animal were still alive. Behind the creature, you notice a black door made out of pumice stone. You decide to walk towards the door to leave the room.

Walk to section 161

159

You choose to open the door on which a tiger is painted. You step into a small room entirely built out of stone plates. You look around the room and see that dead tigers stuffed with straw surround you. The species of tiger are displayed hanging on the walls and are placed on the stone floor in the middle of the small room. A white tiger's fur is lying on the floor next to a couple of broken teeth.

"Poor animals," you say out loud.

In the room's right wall, you see two doors. On each one, two different animals are painted in red. There is a sloth on the left door, and a rat on the right one.

If you want to open the left door, go to section 163

If you prefer opening the right door, walk to section 165

160

Carried by your faithful mount, you are back at Keinu's hideout before you know it. When the man sees you and Kossol alive, you notice two small tears running down his soft cheeks.

"My friend," says the wizard, "you are here! You have completed the two horrifying quests! We, the people of Zaar, are truly blessed to have *The Chosen One* amongst us."

"The honor is mine," you simply answer.

"Come and rest, my friend."

Keinu invites you to savour a delicious meal with fresh spring water. Once again, you tell the old man what happened during your quest, and how you were extremely impressed by Kossol's magical powers.

"It is an incredible horse, isn't it? A wizard friend of mine who specializes in all kinds of animal magic gave Kossol its mighty powers. Long ago, I healed my friend from a terrible illness, so as a token of his gratitude, he turned Kossol into a mighty horse. My friend obviously did a great job!"

"He sure did!" you say laughing.

"Tomorrow, you will have to face your toughest challenge yet: Darkblade himself. He is an extremely powerful sorcerer who mastered black magic, so do not underestimate his might. At night time only, find a way to enter the king's castle, now Darkblade's castle. This will not be an easy task, because the castle is heavily guarded at all times. Once inside, find the main laboratory. Apparently, its doors are magically locked, and I don't know how to open them. Maybe there is a different entrance to it, but if so, I know nothing about it. Inside the laboratory, you will find Darkblade. He is always there at night time doing some incessant experiment to increase his powers. Neutralize him as fast as you can, and come back to me. I will have the secret magical formula ready to be injected into one of his veins."

"What about all the hostages and prisoners?" you ask, perplexed. "I must free them first!"

"You won't need to do that. As soon as we will erase the required part of Darkblade's memory, all evil created by him will vanish forever, and all the people of Zaar will be freed from all aspects of the sorcerer's black magic. Do you understand what I've just said? We will all be FREE again…thanks to you!"

"I understand," you reply. "Thank you for all your advice and everything else. I will now go to sleep, and get some much needed rest before my ultimate quest tomorrow evening."

Continue your journey to section 171

161

You look at the door where a big monkey is painted, and you open it. You step into a tiny room entirely built out of thin stone plates. You immediately see that the room is filled with dead monkeys stuffed with straw. All the species are displayed and are placed everywhere in the room.

"Those animals must have suffered a great deal," you say to yourself.

In the room's left wall, next to a giant gorilla, you notice two doors. On each one, two different animals are painted in red. There is a hyena on the left door, and a puma on the right one.

If you want to open the left door, go to section 166

If you prefer opening the right door, walk to section 168

162

You decide to open the door with a buffalo painted on it. You step into a room looking the same way as the previous one but smaller. In front of you, there is a big buffalo stuffed with straws, standing on the hard floor.

"I wonder where all these stuffed animals come from," you say out loud.

You walk around the small room but don't see anything of interest besides the buffalo. In the right wall, you suddenly notice a closed door with a tiger on it.

"There is nothing more to see here." You decide to go toward the door to leave the room.

Continue your journey to section 159

163

You decide to open the door with the sloth painted on it. You step into a tiny room entirely built out of white rubber but barely bigger than a closet. In front of you, you see a small tree growing out of the rubber. On one of the tree's branches, you notice a baby sloth hanging upside down, and breathing deeply.

"This one is alive!" you say out loud. You pet the little creature as it looks at you with its puffy face, wondering if you have anything good to eat. In the right corner of the tiny room, you notice a slide sloping down and sticking out of the rubber floor. You go sit on the slide made out of an extremely slippery material and let yourself slide down, leaving behind the tiny room and the adorable sloth. But a moment later, you feel a sudden invisible force ejecting you out of the slide, making you fly through a complete darkness. Without any feeling of where you could be, you land on your back in the middle of a tunnel.

Go and reach section 153

164

After opening the door with a jaguar painted on it, you step into a room built exactly like the previous one. You are surprised to see that the room is completely empty. The only detail you notice is a closed steel door in the wall in front of you. After opening the heavy door, you step into some kind of a small closet made out of green rubber. The only thing you notice is a blue door in front of you with a monkey painted on it.

Continue your journey to section 161

165

Suddenly, the white light around you becomes so incredibly bright that you have to close your eyes, blinded by its power. Carefully, you crawl in the direction where you saw the hole. You easily reach it, grabbing the ladder with your hands, your eyes still closed. With great dexterity, you quickly go down the ladder, escaping the blinding light.

Rapidly, you climb down until you reach a room not too far below. The room is full of sand, and small dead bugs looking like tiny sharks lie everywhere. You suddenly notice a door in front of you with the picture of a snake on it.

"Let's get out of this filthy place!"

Run to section 157

166

You look at the door where a hyena is painted, and you open it. You walk into a big triangular room completely built with wood stained in yellow. On the wooden floor, you notice all kinds of strange weapons lying around. Hanging on the walls, you see swords, shields, knives, axes, and bows. You walk towards one of the walls to look at the weapons. Suddenly, a trap opens underneath your feet, and you fall into the darkness of a wide hole!

A moment later, you come out of the hole and fall onto the ground, finding yourself in front of four large stone doors placed one next to another. Curiously again, a different animal has been painted in red on every door.

Hurry to section 159!

167

You grab the left doorknob, and after carefully turning it, you swing the door open. Before you know it, you fall on your knees with three spears piercing your stomach. When you opened the door, you activated a sophisticated mechanism launching three sharp spears in the direction of the door. Unfortunately for you, you never saw them…or felt them coming! Your quest was almost finished, but it does not change anything for you now because you are simply dead.

THE END

168

You decide to open the door with a puma painted on it and walk into a place that you have never seen before. Immediately, you start floating in a very blurry room, having the impression of being under some kind of dirty bluish water. You look all around and see blue and white patches everywhere, filling all the space surrounding you. Your body starts to shake as you are being twisted through the air, finding it more and more difficult to breathe. A tremendous invisible force suddenly pushes you forward into the unknown as your head starts to spin. You feel nauseous and out of control, wanting to escape this other reality...

Brusquely, that same invisible force drops you like a stone as you land on the floor, finding yourself in a different room than before. In front of you, there is a door with a snake painted on it.

Get up and go to section 157

169

You try to open the right door, but it is locked. You try again, applying a pressure with your shoulder against it, but the door still will not budge.

"I can't back down," you say to yourself. "I must open that door!"

With an amazingly powerful spinning back kick, you pulverize the heavy wooden door turning it into a pile of broken boards. You quickly step into a little room only furnished with a large square table made out of sand and eggs. On the table, you see a multicolored parrot made out of wood with its beak wide open.

"What in the world was that noise?" says a voice on your right.

You suddenly notice an older woman sitting on the dusty wooden floor underneath a large window, leaning against a wooden wall. She is reading a thick book while petting a red cat. Fast as lightening, you reach the woman and lift her off the floor. Applying a double arm lock behind her back, you tell her:

"Don't scream if you want to stay in one piece. I am..."

"I know who you are," the woman calmly interrupts. "I am Melza and you are *The Chosen One* sent here by my good friend and work partner Keinu to find the silver power of memory. How I ended up here would be too long to explain, but you must know that I have been a prisoner in this labyrinth since Darkblade built it. Let's make a deal, shall we? Promise to take me away with you from this awful place, and I will tell you where the powder is."

"How do I know that you are not really on Darkblade's side?" you ask the woman. "What proof do I have that you are telling the truth?"

"I have no proof to offer, but if you trust me, I will gain back my freedom and you will get the magical powder that you need."

Reluctantly, you let go of Melza's arms, and say:

"Where is the powder?"

"It is hidden in the parrot's upper throat. Darkblade put it there for his future use...or abuse I should say."

You walk to the bird, put two fingers down its beak, and take out a small transparent test tube filled with a shiny silver powder. Holding the tube between your fingers, you truly feel that Melza told you the truth.

Run as fast as you can to section 170!

170

"Stay close to me and do exactly as I say," you tell Melza.

Suddenly, an old bald druid dressed in a long white robe enters the little room. He is followed by at least ten sand guards armed with bows and long arrows. Starring at you and at Melza, he abruptly yells:

"Guards, take away their lives at once and bring to me the silver powder of memory!"

You tackle the woman to the ground and fall beside her to avoid a bunch of deadly arrows flying your way. Before the massive sandmen can launch another bunch of arrows, you grab Melza and run to the large window.

"Jump through the window and let yourself slide against the wall!" you tell her.

"I can't!" She panics. "I will free-fall and die!"

"No you won't!" You scream. "The labyrinth's structure may be abrupt, but it's a slope. GO!"

"I CAN'T!"

Without wasting more time, you flip Melza through the window and jump right behind her, letting yourself slide down the steep slope. Coming from above, at least five arrows fly right beside your head, barely missing you, but hitting Melza. With horror, you see blood spilling out of her neck where an arrow lodged itself. The woman finds the strength to look at you and smile as she mumbles:

"Put an end to all this violence. It is your destiny. I will pray for you in heaven."

An unbearable sadness fills your heart as you see all signs of life slowly vanishing through her eyes. "Rest in peace," you whisper, looking at her. A second later, the old woman's body starts to become transparent, then turns into sparkles...and finally disappears before your eyes!

A deep pile of sand softens your landing as you hit the ground. You immediately start running forward towards the forest where Kossol is waiting for you. Behind you, you hear a voice screaming:

"Wild beasts, I am once again giving you the gift of life. Bring me back the stranger dead or alive, and find my missing powder! Guards, join them!!"

You turn around to look at the labyrinth's entrance…and cannot believe your eyes! All the wild beasts stuffed with straw that you saw inside are now coming out of the labyrinth in search for you, followed by at least one hundred massive sand guards!!

**If you master the skill of eternal breath and wish to use it,
dive into section 176**

**If you choose to fight the group using your martial arts skills,
propel yourself to section 174**

If you wish to try to call Kossol, scream as loud as you can at section 172

171

You wake up late the next morning, feeling well rested but very hungry. After greeting your host and sampling a wide variety of different foods, you step outside with Keinu to get some fresh air. Together, you walk through the green pastures, talking about tonight's events and hoping for the best.

"How am I supposed to go back to Tibet with an unconscious man in my arms?" you ask Keinu. "As you know, Tibet is a very long way from here!"

"I will send you and Darkblade to Tibet using molecular travel," answers the wizard. "To do so, you will drink a magical potion prepared by me, and I will then inject a similar potion into the sorcerer's neck. Together, you will then find yourselves in front of the lamasery…in no time!"

"Thank you for everything, Keinu. I truly appreciate all your help."

"No, it is I, who thank you," says the old master-wizard as he gives you two little taps in the back.

The night comes very fast, and it seems darker than ever, as if it is hiding a weapon of mass destruction underneath its heavy black coat.

"It's time my friend," says Keinu. "This is your ultimate test. Use all you have learned in Tibet and through your life to guide you during this terrible journey. I will pray for you to be successful, and to come back alive. Kossol will take you to the castle. Be careful…and good luck."

"Thank you. I will come back, I swear it!"

Grabbing the horse's saddle, you jump on its back and yell:

"To Darkblade's castle, Kossol!"

A second later, you are gone, your horse galloping through the air towards an imminent and petrifying danger…

Prepare yourself for section 173!

172

"Kossol!" you yell as loud as you can. "It's now or never!"

In the blink of an eye, the magnificent horse stands in front of you, understanding the gravity of the situation.

"You are truly full of surprises," you tell the animal. Behind you, you notice the numerous guards and wild animals running in your direction.

"Stop them!" screams the bald druid. "I want them both dead!"

You jump on your mount as arrows start flying through the macabre night, and you quickly find yourself high in the air above the labyrinth and its dreadful creatures.

"Hurry Kossol! Back to Keinu's hideout!"

**If this quest is the first you have completed,
continue your journey to section 150**

If you have completed both quests, hurry to section 160!

173

At the speed of mind, you arrive at the castle, looking at it from high above in the sky.

"Kossol, bring us down and land between the bushy trees behind the castle."

A split second later, you and your mount hide behind the castle amongst very tall and extremely bushy trees. You jump off your horse and say:

"Wait for me here Kossol and make sure that no one sees you. I should call for you soon."

As if it is telling you to be careful, the splendid animal slowly rubs its head against your shoulders, licking your arm at the same time.

"Don't worry, my friend, I will be back soon enough," you tell Kossol.

You run to the castle's back wall and hide behind a large bush. There, you notice that the back wall is built with small irregular stones bulging out of it, making an eventual climb easy for a person with your training. You look up the wall and suddenly notice a small window very high above the ground. A light comes through it.

"I wonder if there would be a chance of getting inside the castle through its only doors at the front," you ask yourself.

With that idea in mind, you start crawling in the long grass while going around the castle. Staying on your stomach, you finally reach a point where you can see the castle's main doors without being seen. In front of the entrance, you see twelve soldiers armed with heavy swords and bows guarding the doors. From time to time an individual appears, dressed in an ample red robe with a hood covering the head and some kind of red cloth covering the face up but not the eyes. You hear that individual giving orders to the twelve soldiers.

"That's their captain. Now, how am I going to get inside this fortress?"

If you master the skill of invisibility, become invisible at section 175

If you choose to go back where you came from and climb the back wall to reach the enlightened window, climb your way up to section 177

If you wish to fight the twelve guards to get in the castle, fight at section 178

If you have a captain's robe and wish to put it on to fake your identity, walk to section 179

174

You propel yourself forward, jumping extremely high into the air. You land on a black puma, kicking the animal in the face and sending it flying into the nearby creek. Powerful as a tornado, you quickly turn around, avoiding a jumping lion, and throwing it against five massive guards.

"That's for the poor Melza!" you yell at the group.

"And that's for being a fool," says a familiar voice.

A painful electric current suddenly lifts you off the ground, shaking you in every direction. From the sky, you see the bald druid playing with you like if you were a puppet. The man stares at you and says:

"Now, I will feed you to my artificial animals!"

He drops you just above a huge polar bear and a hungry jaguar, but you smash into the wild beasts with your feet, kicking them on the nose and breaking their jaws at the same time. But a second later, you find yourself lying on your stomach...with six arrows between your shoulder blades.

"You are certainly a very tough opponent, but I told you that I would feed you to my beasts!"

Those are the last words you hear.

THE END

175

From your hidden point, you stare at your enemies as you start shaking every molecule of your body extremely fast. By moving your molecules so amazingly fast, you are becoming more and more difficult to see. A few seconds later, you completely disappear, now totally invisible. You get up and walk to the main entrance. You stop in front of the door waiting for it to open, staring at the twelve soldiers guarding the tall entrance. After a short while, the soldier's captain appears and says:

"We are all in position and ready to leave for the invasion of the new territory. I will go ask our master Darkblade when he wants us to move forward."

Two massive guards open the doors, and you finally enter the palace, following the captain's footsteps. You step into a huge ballroom with barely any lights and walk forward. The room is empty, free of any furniture, and the walls are covered with some kind of slimy liquid. You also notice cylindrical pylons everywhere along the stone walls.

Following the captain, you reach a very wide and long staircase. Quickly, you walk up the heavy stairs covered with a red velvet carpet until you reach the top. You follow a wide and empty corridor, admiring the very high ceiling painted with bright colours. The captain suddenly stops as you reach the end of the corridor. Facing a massive stone door at least three times your height and five times your width, you hear the captain saying the words *MA-KE-BE-DA-LA*. Instantaneously, the door opens without a sound as you follow the captain.

Now inside the laboratory, you take a good look at it. It is strongly enlightened with a familiar artificial blue light and has only one small window high above the ground. The floor is covered with pretty yellowish and polished marble plates, but the walls are simply built with big irregular stones bulging out of it. There are big cylindrical pylons all around the laboratory, and wooden shelves fixed only to the back wall. On those shelves you see all the possible instruments, liquids, powers, roots, and other gear that a druid or wizard could dream of having. Your attention shifts to the middle of the laboratory in front of a very long and narrow table where the captain is conversing with a man who is quite tall. The man is dressed in a long darkish robe, has barely any hair and holds a well-crafted staff. The only words you here are:

"Yes, my master."

Without adding a word, the captain abruptly walks out of the room, leaving you alone with his master. As you become visible again, you slowly walk towards the middle of the laboratory, approaching the tall man who stands with his back to you.

Get ready for section 180!

176

You run to the nearby creek and jump into the cold water, avoiding a deadly confrontation with numerous enemies quickly closing in on you. Immediately, you take some water in your mouth and start extracting the air from it, filling up your lungs with oxygen while releasing the water through your lips and taking more fresh water in. After a few seconds of swimming towards the bottom of the creek, you flip upside down in the water and look up towards the surface. All around the creek, you see the wild animals, the massive guards, and the bald druid staring at the water, probably wondering when you were going to show yourself.

"I have a feeling that all these creatures are going to wait for me a very long time," you think to yourself.

As you swim deeper and deeper, a weak light grabs your attention below. You swim towards that light and quickly notice that it comes from an underwater tunnel to your left. You keep swimming and enter the tunnel full of tiny fish. As you progress forward, the light in the tunnel slowly intensifies.

After swimming for about thirty minutes, you finally reach the surface. You look all around you and realize that you are in the middle of a large pond in the very same forest where you left Kossol. You swim to shore and quickly get out of the cold water.

"Kossol!" you say loud enough for the horse to hear you. "I am over here!"

In a second, your stunning mount is in front of you, licking your hand, and waiting for your command.

"Our quest here is completed. Let's go back to Keinu's hideout."

In no time, you were once again up in the air, crossing the sky at tremendous speed towards the master-wizard's hideout.

If this quest is the first one you have completed,
continue your journey to section 150

If you have completed both quests, hurry to section 160

177

"Trying to force my way in through the main doors would be a big mistake. Once inside, I wouldn't know where to go anyway, and would probably be surrounded by numerous guards before I could reach Darkblade. Let's find another way in."

You crawl back where you came from until you reach the back wall. You then look up again, and see a bluish light coming through the small window that you noticed before.

"That's my cue."

Being an expert climber, you start climbing the thick stone wall, pushing well with your legs, and keeping a tight hold on those small rocks bulging out from everywhere.

"Keep your body close to the wall at all times, and stop focusing on pulling yourself up! Use your legs to progress."

You smile as you remember what the High Priest from Tibet used to tell you when you were under his tutelage. In no time, you reach the small window. Immediately, you secure a solid grip on its edge before taking a look inside. From what you see, you are staring at some kind of laboratory.

"Maybe this is the laboratory I am looking for. I really hope it is."

You pull yourself inside without making any noise. With great agility and speed, you climb down the wall faster than a spider, you reach the bottom and hide behind a thick cylindrical pylon. Now inside the laboratory, you take a good look at it. It is strongly enlightened with a familiar artificial blue light and has only one small window high above the ground. The floor is covered with pretty yellowish and polished marble plates, but the walls are built simply with small irregular stones bulging out of them. There are big cylindrical pylons all around the laboratory and wooden shelves fixed only to the back wall. On those shelves you see all the possible instruments, liquids, powers, roots, and other gear that a druid or wizard needs. Your attention shifts to the middle of the laboratory in front of a very long and narrow table where a very tall man is mixing a green bubbly potion. The man is dressed in a long darkish robe, has barely any hair, and holds a well-crafted staff.

"I know who you are," you say to yourself.

You slowly walk towards the middle of the laboratory, approaching the tall man who stands with his back to you.

Prepare yourself for section 180!

178

"I will fight my way into the castle," you quickly decide.

You charge towards the main doors, but before you can even reach them, two throwing knives hit you right in the chest. You fall on your back, not able to breathe. The last person you see is a woman dressed in a long red robe, standing over you.

"I believe your mission ends right here," she says to you.

Unfortunately, she is correct.

THE END

179

"Why didn't I think of this before?"

Without making any noise, you take out the captain's robe that you kept in your backpack and quickly put it on, covering your head and face appropriately. Cautiously, you then walk towards the main entrance and stop when you reach the soldiers guarding the doors.

"I need one of you to come with me to see our master," you order the group.

"Of course captain," replies a high-ranking soldier. "Guards, let us in."

Two massive soldiers open the double doors as you enter the palace, following the high-ranking soldier. You step into a huge ballroom with barely any lights and walk forward. The room is empty, free of any furniture, and the walls are covered with some kind of slimy liquid. You also notice tall cylindrical pylons everywhere along the stone walls.

Following the soldier, you reach a very wide and long staircase. Very quickly, you walk up the heavy stairs covered with a red velvet carpet until you reach the top. You follow a wide and empty corridor, admiring the very high ceiling painted with bright colours. The soldier suddenly stops as you reach the end of the corridor. Facing a massive stone door at least three times your height and five times your width, you tell the soldier:

"Open the door and leave at once."

The soldier says the words *MA-KE-BE-DA-LA*. Instantaneously, the door opens as the man leaves. You walk into a large laboratory, almost counting your steps.

Now inside, you take a good look at the laboratory. It is strongly lightened with a familiar artificial blue light and has only one small window high above the ground. The floor is covered with pretty yellowish and polished marble plates, but the walls are built simply with small irregular stones bulging out of them. There are big cylindrical pylons all around the laboratory, and wooden shelves fixed only to the back wall. On those shelves you see all the possible instruments, liquids, powers, roots, and other gear that a druid or wizard could dream of having. Your attention shifts to the middle of the laboratory in front of a very long and narrow table where a very tall man is crushing some roots with a special tool. The man is dressed in a long darkish robe, has barely any hair, and holds a well-crafted staff.

"I have a feeling I know who that man is."

You slowly walk towards the middle of the laboratory, approaching the tall man who is standing with his back facing you.

Carefully walk to section 180!

180

Before you can reach the tall man, he slowly turns around to face you, his eyes very deep and motionless, his voice echoing within the entire laboratory:

"I have been expecting you, *Chosen One*."

A cold chill runs down your spine as you try to keep a complete composure of yourself.

"I am Darkblade...as I am sure you know by now."

For the first time, you see the sorcerer's face. You immediately notice his white chalky skin and crooked nose. His little mouth with non-existent lips is filled with black short teeth. His wide jaw and chin slanted forward seem bigger due to his tiny ears and low forehead covered with just a few scattered hairs. But, first and foremost, you almost feel hypnotized by his oval red flaming eyes diving into yours.

"Your reputation precedes you, *Chosen One*, and I must say that I am quite impressed by all your accomplishments. Even in the presence of my

blue artificial light that inhibited you from using some of your mental powers, you were still able to stay alive while finding the silver powder of memory, and the great magical book of spells. This is why it saddens me to have to eliminate such a prodigious opponent as yourself. You always gave me a new challenge to look for. Unfortunately, there is no place in Zaar for the both of us, so you must go...to hell!"

"What if we both rule as partners?" you ask Darkblade.

"You don't expect me to believe such pathetic lie, do you? I am well aware of your mission and will do whatever it takes to stop you...once and for all!"

The sorcerer suddenly blows on you with such force that you fly half way across the laboratory before hitting the floor. Now walking towards you, Darkblade goes on saying:

"I know that you were ordered not to kill me, so now you will understand the advantage that I have over you!"

If you master the skill of the heavenly shield, propel yourself to section 182

If you have the magical skill of ice bolt, hurry to section 184

If have the fire jet skill, run to section 186

If you know the skill of paralysis, get ready for section 188

If you don't have any of the above skills, fight for your life at section 190

181

For a quick second, Darkblade inadvertently turns his back on you to somehow put the flames out.

"This is my chance," you tell yourself.

One tremendous spring brings you high into the air, right above Darkblade's head. As you fall down, you strike your opponent at the back of the neck with the edge of your hand. The evil man does not even realize what hit him as he abruptly topples over on to his stomach, knocked out unconscious.

"Let's put the fire out and leave this place with the sorcerer."

Go to section 185!

182

Very quickly, you breathe to feel the energy around you and in the air. You feel it penetrating every molecule of your body, filling it up completely. You then direct it around your forearm while executing a large circular movement with your arm. In a blink of an eye, you are holding the impenetrable shield of heaven.

"You think that you will be able to stop me with that toy of yours?" laughs Darkblade.

"Yes," you tell the sorcerer, staring at him with great determination.

"We shall see," says Darkblade.

He immediately throws a powerful fireball in your direction. To his great surprise, you easily stop the projectile with your shield. Launching a new attack, the evil sorcerer sends tremendous ice bolts straight to your head, but you avoid being hit by simply lifting up your shield. Without any warning, you jump high in the air toward Darkblade to hit him with your shield, but you miss as he steps back.

"You are more clever than I thought," says the sorcerer.

Through his eyes, he brusquely shoots flaming arrows at you, but once again his attacks are no match for your shield.

Trust your instincts at all times

The High Priest's voice echoes in your head once more. Instinctively, you make a move totally unexpected by Darkblade. Fast as lightening, you throw your shield towards the sorcerer's body. The shield whistles through the air as a sharp dreadful blade and smashes into Darkblade's abdomen, throwing him against the hard floor, and knocking the air out of him. Without wasting a second, you launch forward and take back your shield. Holding it firmly, you swing it at the sorcerer's temple, trying to knock him unconscious, but the evil sorcerer brusquely turns into a small tornado, lifting you off the floor, and sending you flying across the laboratory.

"I will now blind you before sending you to meet your new friend Melza!" says Darkblade.

Abruptly, ten dangerous white rays come out of his fingers as you raise the shield in front of your face. Following a deep intuition, you tilt the shield into an awkward angle, and make the white rays rebound directly in Darkblade's face, blinding him momentarily. Dropping your shield, you jump forward and strike the man with your fist across the chin. A second later, he is lying unconscious at your feet.

Hurry to section 185!

183

Immediately, you throw many more fire jets at the long table, and at the wooden shelves fixed to the back wall, burning all kinds of gears.

"ENOUGH!" yells Darkblade.

Furious beyond words, he suddenly turns into a gigantic snake, longer than the width of the laboratory.

"YOU WILL NOW PAY FOR WHAT YOU HAVE DONE!" whistles the snake.

It launches towards you, but you jam your foot straight into its eye. The snake suddenly turns around and hits you with its powerful tail, sending you flying to the other side of the room. You crash into the hard wall and fall flat on your back, screaming with pain, blood spilling out of your ears. The last thing you see is the snake's giant mouth closing on your body.

THE END

184

You look straight into Darkblade's eyes, focusing on them while opening a huge flow of magic inside of you. You feel the ice coming to the surface of your hands, ready to be used. As fast as the wind, you throw three consecutive ice bolts towards the evil sorcerer, but he annihilates your attack by turning the ice into tiny snow flakes!

"Is that the best can do?" asks the sorcerer, obviously mocking you.

He suddenly opens his mouth and sends a ravaging fire jet in your direction. You barely have the time to dive on the floor to avoid being severely burned.

"Now my turn," you whisper.

In a dazzling spring, you jump into the air towards Darkblade and land right behind him. Spinning around, the sorcerer pulls out a knife and tries to slash your throat. In a very rapid reflex, you sweep the armed hand and throw the evil man over your hip, smashing him into the floor's plates and breaking three of them. Momentarily dizzy, Darkblade turns on his stomach to catch his breath, but you jump on his back, pinning him to the ground while applying a guillotine choke around his throat. Nevertheless, he manages to bite your hand and to free himself from your grip by throwing you to your side. Unexpectedly, before making contact with the floor, you turn towards your opponent and throw two enormous ice bolts straight on his legs, freezing him completely.

"That was quite a challenge," you say out loud while getting back on your feet. You stare at Darkblade for a short moment. He now looks like an ugly ice sculpture.

Run to section 185!

185

You grab the sorcerer and throw him onto your shoulders.

"I must get out of this place…fast!"

As soon as you walk out of the laboratory, you meet face to face with a group of soldiers led by their captain, a short and strong woman. Immediately, you yell at them:

"Step aside if you want your master to live!"

Totally caught off guard, the astonished soldiers simply stare at you, not able to make the slightest movement.

"You want to risk putting his life in jeopardy because of your foolishness?" you ask the group. "Let us pass and he will live! You want be held responsible for his death?"

Slowly, the captain and her soldiers step aside to let you pass.

"Try anything to stop me and your master will regret it with his life," you tell them.

In no time, you reach the main entrance. As you step outside the castle, you notice an army of soldiers and high-ranking officers staring at you in disbelief. Without waiting, you scream at them:

"I am holding your master hostage! Try anything to stop us from leaving this place, and you will be responsible for his death! You want him to live? Then step aside at once!"

"You are bluffing," says a captain on your right. "You would not dare to kill our master."

"Would you be foolish enough to take such a risk, captain?" suddenly asks a voice coming from high above the ground. You look above your head and see an older man dressed in a long white robe, floating in the air and looking at you with a big smile on his face.

Continue your journey to section 191

186

You look at the table behind Darkblade and notice a green liquid bubbling in a glass jar above a huge candle. Focusing on that jar, you open a huge flow of magic inside of you, feeling the fire coming to the surface of your hands, making them hot and steamy. In a single and precise movement, you throw a long fire jet through the air, crashing it into the jar.

"NO!" screams the evil sorcerer as he turns and sees the damage.

If you wish to use your martial arts skills to attack him,
jump to section 181

If you choose to set more of his things on fire, do it at section 183

187

As you fly through the air, you try to avoid the collision with Darkblade by twisting your body in any way possible way, but you cannot avoid the impact. You crash into the sorcerer, and die instantly. But it did not have to be this way…

By moving uncontrollably through the air, you unconsciously opened your arms to your opponent before smashing into him. Grabbing the occasion, Darkblade viciously kicked you in the solar plexus, pulverizing it and killing you in a split second. But it did not have to be this way…

THE END

188

Once again, Darkblade blows on you with amazing force, sending you crashing against a wall. You hit a rock with your head and feel tiny drops of blood going down the side of your face. You fall to the ground, faking unconsciousness. Slowly, Darkblade walks up to you and says:

"That was too easy. I thought that you were going to be a lot tougher than this!"

Inadvertently, he picks you off the ground to look at your face, but drops you and falls flat on his back onto the marble floor. He is completely awake but paralyzed from head to toe because you just struck a vital point on his chest with your index finger.

"That was way too easy!" you tell the sorcerer. "I would off never thought that a tough guy like yourself could fall for such an easy trick. Now I will put you to sleep. Sweet dreams!"

In a swift movement, you knock him unconscious by pressing on

another pressure point. You grab Darkblade and say:
   "Now let's get out of here!"

It's time to go to section 185!

189

At great speed, you fly towards Darkblade, preparing for the impact. When you are about to smash into him, you extend your legs, and with amazing power you kick your opponent above the knees to avoid killing him. The sorcerer immediately falls on his back, holding his legs, and screaming with great pain.

"You won't have to suffer much longer," you tell Darkblade.

Without adding a word, you jump on top of him and apply a quick pressure to a vital point behind his head. Instantaneously, the evil sorcerer stops moving, now completely unconscious.

Propel yourself to section 185!

190

"Good bye, *Chosen One*," says Darkblade.

The sorcerer drops a black rock on the marble floor and turns it into a horrible beast twice as big as you. It has the head of a lizard, the body of a tiger, the tail of a huge beaver, and the legs of a crocodile. Slowly, the beast walks in your direction, staring at you, obviously very hungry.

"This creature can't run fast nor jump high because of its short legs," you observe. "I therefore have a certain advantage over it."

You start running towards the back wall, followed by the hungry beast. You notice Darkblade observing the scene with a curious eye, obviously amused by what is happening. You suddenly change direction and walk towards the long table, purposely letting the creature close the distance between the two of you.

Understanding your strategy, Darkblade propels himself in your direction, but it is too late. You launch towards the long table and grab the jar with the green bubbly liquid. You immediately throw it at the beast and say:

"Enjoy your meal!"

The creature grabs the jar full of liquid, and swallows it immediately.

"NO!" screams the sorcerer.

A second later, the beast explodes in tiny pieces before your own eyes, the shock of the explosion throwing you forward directly towards Darkblade!

If you try to avoid the collision with Darkblade, fly to section 187

**If you want to smash into him,
prepare yourself for the impact at section 189**

191

"It's the powerful flying sorcerer!" yells a captain. "Bow to him or die by his hand!"

You see all the soldiers and officers go down on their knees, prostrating themselves in front of the old man. Looking at you with admiration, the man says:

"My name is Dell, and I am the one who made the crucial prophecy about you one hundred years ago. My heart is filled with joy knowing that Darkblade is neutralized and that your mission is almost completed. I am greatly impressed to see that you didn't even have to use the magical words *Ma-Ke-Be-Da-La* to open the laboratory's doors. From the bottom of my heart, I wish to thank you for saving Zaar and the other magical worlds from a dreadful destiny. You truly are our savior, and the people of Zaar will be grateful to you forever."

"Thank you kindly," you simply tell the old man. "I must now leave to complete my mission, but I will be back to celebrate Zaar's freedom with its people."

"We will be waiting for your return," says Dell.

You call Kossol and an instant later the beautiful black horse is standing in front of you. After throwing Darkblade on your horse, you say:

"Let's go back to Keinu's hideout and finish this mission!"

You jump on Kossol's saddle as the black mount throws itself across the dark sky, braving the strong winds of the night.

Continue your journey to section 192

192

Travelling at the speed of mind, you reach Keinu's hideout in no time. Once again, the master-wizard greets you with open arms, screaming with joy:

"You are back! You are alive and Darkblade is with you! I knew you would be successful in your mission. Congratulations, my dear friend!"

Looking at the unconscious sorcerer, Keinu then adds: "Let's take him inside before he wakes up."

You grab the unconscious man and drag him into the hideout as the master-wizard says:

"Using my magical book of spells, various ingredients, and the silver powder of memory, I created a magical potion that will be injected into Darkblade's neck. Immediately, all his powers, creations, curses and magical spells will then vanish, freeing Zaar from all his evil. As well, every piece of information concerning the Black Death formula will be forever erased from his memory. When Darkblade will awake, he will only remember being Rekken, the healer druid who always wanted to help others and to be recognized as a great druid."

Inside the hideout, you put Darkblade in a large wooden armchair as Keinu grabs a syringe containing the magical potion. Grabbing the sorcerer by the neck, the master-wizard says:

"Let's not waste any more time."

Before Keinu could jab the needle into the neck and administer the potion, Darkblade suddenly opens his eyes, and yells:

"NEVER SURRENDER!!!"

**If you wish Keinu to jab the needle into Darkblade's neck,
step into section 193**

If you want to try to put the sorcerer asleep, walk to section 194

193

You quickly jump aside to let Keinu inject the potion into the sorcerer's body. Immediately, the evil man rushes to his feet, blowing strongly on you and throwing the master-wizard against a wall. Without a warning, two white freezing rays come out of his eyes, turning you and Keinu into ice sculptures. Greatly satisfied, the sorcerer says:

"I know you can still see and hear," says the evil sorcerer, "so listen to this: I will not allow you or anybody else to change my destiny. I will be the king of all the magical worlds, and their people will obey me. Now say goodbye."

A horrific feeling fills you as you see Darkblade picking up a gigantic mace from a nearby table.

"Now I will reduce you both to pieces," says the master of black magic.

A second later, a dark curtain falls forever over your eyes. You were so close of finishing your mission! You did not listen to your instinct.

THE END

194

Immediately, you strike Darkblade at the base of his neck to put him back to sleep.

"I told you that we were running out of time," says Keinu with an amazing calm in his voice. "Let's do this."

With great dexterity, you see him stabbing the syringe into Darkblade's neck and slowly injecting the liquid.

"It's done," says Keinu. "The potion will now enter the blood stream and do its work. Your mission here is accomplished." Putting his hand on your shoulder, he whispers:

"Thank you once again for everything! You saved us all."

"Thank you for helping me out," you tell Keinu. "Without your help, I don't know what the outcome of my mission would have been."

"You must now go to Tibet," says the master-wizard. "I prepared a traveling potion which will send you and Darkblade to the entrance of the Tibetan lamasery. There, you will meet all your old friends, including the High Priest. But remember that the potion's effects cannot last very long. About fifteen minutes after your arrival, you will travel back home."

"I understand. Thank you for everything, Master Keinu. I will be back, I promise."

"I know you will. Now it's time for you to drink this."

You take the glass handed to you by Keinu, and you see a blue sparkling potion inside it.

"It smells awful!" you say to yourself.

You quickly drink it as Keinu injects the same traveling potion into one of Darkblade's shoulders. Your vision becomes slightly blurry. Keinu tells you:

"Goodbye, my dear friend. Thank you again for everything, and send my regards to my good friend the High Priest."

Immediately, you and Darkblade are sucked in a powerful spiral that throws you in every direction, shakes you like tiny seashells in the middle of a furious ocean. But this strange roller coaster does not last very long. A moment later, you find yourself standing in front of the lamasery, your second home, with Darkblade lying at your feet.

Continue your journey to section 195

195

You are about to grab Darkblade and throw him on your shoulders when you suddenly notice familiar monks running out of the lamasery.

"My friends!" you say out loud.

In no time, you are surrounded by all your Tibetan friends, your second family, now greeting you warmly and hugging you. At the entrance of the lamasery, you see a tall bald man coming out and smiling.

"The High Priest!" you say with excitement.

You approach the grandiose man who greets you very warmly.

"Welcome back! I knew you would succeed in this very difficult mission. We all knew it. Now all the magical worlds are saved thanks to you."

"No, it's thanks to you," you tell the High Priest. "You are the one who taught me all the skills I know, and who trusted me for this perilous mission."

Surrounded by all your great friends, you walk into the lamasery, answering everyone's questions about how your mission went, and telling the High Priest about all the amazing people you have met. After a short while, you tell your second family:

"My friends, I will unfortunately have to leave very soon, but I give you my word that I will be back to spend more time with all of you." Looking at the High Priest, you bow to him and say:

"Master, thank you once again for saving my life nine years ago, and for pouring your wonderful knowledge into me."

"You are more than worthy of it, my friend. Now go in peace, and come back to us soon."

After saying goodbye to everyone, you notice that your body slowly starts to disappear. Then, you are sucked in a familiar powerful spiral, throwing in every direction, and shaking you like a leaf in a strong wind. A moment later, you find yourself standing in front of your home, safe and happy.

"This was a marvelous adventure!" you tell yourself. "Thank God I'm alive. I should now get some rest before going back to Zaar to visit all my new friends like I said I would, and celebrate their freedom with them!"

CONGRATULATIONS!

YOU HAVE COMPLETED

YOUR

MISSION!

NOW

GET READY

TO

DETERMINE YOUR DESTINY!

YOUR NEXT ADVENTURE

AWAITS YOU!

ABOUT THE AUTHOR

As a young boy, Jeff Storm did not really enjoy reading. He could not relate to most books offered to him and quickly got bored reading them. One day his mother introduced him to all sorts of action packed books written by the elusive French writer Henri Vernes and the American icon Robert Ludlum. Jeff was hooked. He loved the martial arts sequences, the good triumphing over evil, and the bandits being stopped. He felt a strong connection to the stories, sometimes imagining he was the hero catching the bad guys. As he read those books, he had a vision: someday, he would start his own collection of books where the reader is the hero of the story... and he did, adding many incredible twists to his outstanding and unique work!

Besides being a passionate writer, Jeff Storm is a dedicated teacher with many years of experience under his belt. "I love children and find that every day, I am learning something new from them. If I can inspire my students to use their creativity and imagination in a positive way in order to reach their personal goals and have the success they want, I have done my job."